About the author

Nicholas Royle is a Professor of English at the University of Sussex and lives in Seaford. He has written numerous books on literature and critical theory, including *Telepathy and Literature*, *The Uncanny*, *E. M Forster*, and the influential textbook *An Introduction to Literature, Criticism and Theory* (with Andrew Bennett). *Quilt* is his first novel.

QUILT

NICHOLAS ROYLE

Myriad Editions

First published in 2010 by
Myriad Editions
59 Lansdowne Place
Brighton BN3 1FL

www.MyriadEditions.com

3 5 7 9 10 8 6 4 2

A CIP catalogue record for this book is available from
the British Library.

ISBN: 978-0-9562515-4-1

Printed on FSC-accredited paper by
Cox & Wyman Limited, Reading, UK

For Jinan

Then certain Shrouds that muttered head to head
Came and were gone.

W. B. Yeats

Part One

In the middle of the night the phone rings, over and over, but I don't hear it. First it is the hospital, then the police.

Ω

– These things happen from time to time, my father says.

He is lying on the bed, his single bed alongside the other which, still made up, was my mother's, dying two years earlier, and the covers are off and I am trying to get him up and dressed, ready for hospital, but I'm weeping. Tears are streaming down my face making it difficult to see. Unenvisaged, embarrassing. Until now I have managed to remain quite calm, like him. I discussed the case over the phone with the doctor and agreed the best thing would be to get him into hospital where they could make him more comfortable.

– If it's possible to persuade your dad, see what you can do, I know old folk don't necessarily want to shift.

And for all the antiquarian power of his habits he could always amaze me, turn out to have been thinking, or not, entirely elsewhere, for years impossible to get him to go somewhere, come out for a drink, walk by the sea, drive down the country lanes over the hills. I didn't expect him to agree but he did without the faintest remonstrance:

– Yes, take me to the hospital.

He's lying on the bed and he is my flesh, so simple, his body mine, and so difficult, so com-pli-cated he'll say shortly in a portmanteau coming apart at the seams, just when it will have become to my mind most straightforward, so deluded. Give up the thought of the sentence, he seems to tell me, and I am in his grip, he mine, here and from now on, I prop him up, help him sit, help him remove his bedclothes and get him dressed, 'stertorous' is the wrong word but hangs in the air, a signpost to how the most ordinary thing, getting dressed, becomes impracticable fateful tangled up with words and images from a song or book, the grotesque persnicketiness of Edgar Allan Poe, the stertorous breathing of Monsieur Valdemar, figure of impossible, resuscitated putrefaction. It hangs in the air like a silent spy-plane, shadowshow of gallows. That is where living backwards begins: to pronounce dead is to murder, he wrote. All the time the other bed, by her, my father and I all the time aware, though we do not exchange a syllable, unoccupied.

Yesterday I called the doctor in, he asked my father if it would be possible to go upstairs so that he could examine him on the bed and we all went up together, one by one, three bears, me at the back, the doctor in the middle, each of us holding onto the handrail as we went, the doctor remarking with admiration on its crafting, smooth but knotty trunk of a young pine fallen in the garden years ago meticulously bolted to the stairway wall by my father. Solid *silva*, yes, *silva silvam silvae*, the way words twinkle to others' uses, other to her, solid flesh, melting into dew, slivering into you. My father makes to lie down on his bed but the doctor asks him to lie down on the *other* bed, because it is closer to the window and he'll be able to see better. My father is nonplussed, looking over at it he says:

– But that was my wife's bed.

My wife, he says, pronouncing the words very carefully, his speech become fuzzy, especially in the preceding few days, and he strives to overcome it, I can hear the struggle. At innumerable moments in the past he has referred to her as *me wife*, in deliberate loving lapse of propriety, that was me wife's bed, but he doesn't venture it now, we seem to be embarked on some new phase of language. For some days there has been an eerie formality, an explicitness, almost disembodied, in referring to his anatomy and bodily functions, urinating, retraction of the penis, excreting, liquid stools, incontinence, as if this new emphasis on the proper heralds some strange homecoming, the rending mystery of my father. Is there fear and confusion or only loving respect, even awe when he objects, as if to say: But I cannot lie down there, that was my wife's bed. Yet the doctor insists on that bed, it is closer to the window, he says, he'll be able to see better, to see to see, what is it, magically thinking, my father complies.

But now it is today, nearly twenty-four hours later, and we say nothing about the other bed, unoccupied, constantly in our minds.

No, not stertorous, rather *wheezeful*, softer, gulping, an immeasurably beautiful strange ancient fish glopping glooping groping grasping rasping for air, at air, sitting up, slowly so slowly to get dressed, article by article, until the socks, I am dressing my father for the first time in my life, his, due to him melting to me all his body mine, mining me, me father. A miner, yes, that thought is never far away. Underground, he carries it within him, for three years during the Second World War a coalminer day after day deep down in the dark and apparently relishing it, sheer subterranean strength, coming up for air at the end of the day face blackened, hot shower, then tea at his digs, a couple of pints at the local, and bed, then before dawn down again into the earth, mole of my life. It's as I help him dress now I have this searing sensation, smell and feel and look of his body mine, mined out, to have and to hold, every article exhausting and he has to rest, catch or fall back seeking breath respite resources from somewhere unrecognisable. He insists on a vest, shirt and two pullovers even though it is almost the end of July, a hot summer's day. We get to the socks, he is lying down and his feet calloused alien corn swollen, one of them worryingly red, a rash that runs up over his right foot to above the ankle. I haven't been aware of it till now, something else to be looked at in the hospital. I inch on the little soft grey cotton socks for him and the tears begin trickling down my cheeks. I try to conceal this, it is not the place for crying, not in the presence of my father, he does not weep, he whom, yes, incredibly only now for the first time it flashes, I have never seen weep, and he's evidently not about to start now. But I'm blinded: the tears are pouring out of my face. Why merely this word, *tears* or *teardrops*, but no others, like Eskimo snow lexemes? Why not a new language invented every time? What's pouring out of my face has never happened before.

I've succeeded in getting him dressed and can begin to negotiate the business of getting him downstairs and out to the car and drive him to the hospital but I cannot see anything, with all this streaming. I have to tell him, I have to bring myself under control, the thought steadies me:

– I love you, Dad, I say, now standing up between his bed and hers, holding him by the hand.

– I love you too, mate, he says, and the tears flow from me with renewed force, impossible to restrain, strain stain in tears. My father says: don't worry, it's alright. Or he doesn't, no, not that exactly. The precise words are delivered as if from such an unfathomable distance I hardly recognise them:

– These things happen from time to time.

Not even his body which seems, in the wake of this remark, transported to another world, ventriloquism of his heart's desire, not even his body knowing or himself, as if there could be another voice, a strange guardian of my father now remarking that these things happen from time to time; it doesn't occur to me to ask him to clarify, the words might be dreamed, spoken in some walk-on part, picked up snatch on the radio. I came here yesterday, a couple of hundred miles across country, to be with him because in the past week or so, since last seeing him, I had been in regular contact with the doctor and neighbours and gathered from them, as well as from daily telephone conversations with him, a sense of his having significantly declined. A farmer's wife down the lane told me over the phone a couple of days ago:

– He doesn't have long by the look of him, your dad.

I help him sit and stand, finally, and we make our way downstairs. I collect a few things, a couple of books, a notepad, some money, mobile phone. Together we put his jacket on and attempt the shoes, but his feet seem swollen and his slippers are easier. Unspoken sense once more of a slip in the proper course of events, wearing slippers outside, these things happen from time to time. Hobbling out to the car, leaning on me step by step, a month ago he was mowing all the lawns, fit as you like. I help him lower himself into the passenger seat, both of us knowing he never likes to be in a car unless he's driving. Only two days ago he was still making it down to the local shop to collect his newspaper: he's too weak for that now.

I bring the car right up to the hospital entrance, find a wheelchair and ease him into it, stow him in the entrance way next to a large aquarium while I go to park the car. Then I wheel him through to the ward where a nurse welcomes us. We're led to a room in which there are two other patients, a man who is blind and another who, I'll later be informed, has learning disabilities. A couple of nurses shift and winch my father, after a struggle, onto a bed.

– The doctor on duty will come in half an hour or so and have a proper look at him, says one of the nurses pleasantly. Then they leave.

– Things are becoming so com-pli-cated, my father tells me, with a piercing smile of resignation.

And he is right, so viciously true, even though I want to tell him: no, this is simplifying things, it makes sense to be in the hospital, they'll be able to examine you and with luck make you feel more comfortable, we need to find out what's going on, and what can be done to make you stronger and better. But I can't speak. I'm on the verge of streaming tears again. Translucent soldiers lining up, throwing themselves out without parachutes, come from some unknown zone I am struggling like a fish on land to grasp. What to talk about in this simple, abject desolation of a hospital, his body in a foreign bed, mine in a chair alongside? We watch the blindman: two words in the dark and wide, 'blind man', collide. In silence we watch him make his way without a hitch to the lavatory and back.

– No need to turn the light on in there, I'm fine, nurse, he says.

The other man restless, sitting on his bed in a dressing-gown, then walking about a bit, then sitting on his bed again. My father needs some new underwear and pyjamas. His incontinence, lack of time to get any washing done before coming to the hospital. Sentences stop, leak, caught, soil themselves short.

– I'll go and buy some new underwear for you while we're waiting for the doctor, I tell him. And he tells me about the one and only satisfactory brand and style of underpants and points out, with an ironic smile, that there are none to be had in the local town: I must drive to a specialist, old-fashioned hosiery shop in a village on the coast, about twelve miles away.

Ω

The ray lurks, impenetrably, around the origins of philosophy. In Plato, for example, it occupies the space of something like *déjà vu*, it disturbs thinking, dislocating

9

the question of virtue. The ray seems to figure what is magical and uncanny about philosophy. Socrates asks Meno what is virtue. But what Meno already knows, before their first meeting, is that Socrates is not Socrates, he is not purely or simply himself, there is something of the ray about him.

– Even before I met you, says Meno, they told me that, in plain truth, you are a perplexed man yourself and reduce others to perplexity. You are exercising magic and witchcraft upon me, you are exactly like the flat stingray that one meets in the sea. Whenever anyone comes into contact with it, it numbs him, and that is the sort of thing that you seem to be doing to me now. My mind and my lips are literally numb, and I have nothing to reply to you.

– You're a real rascal, Socrates replies. You nearly took me in.

Apparently realising that Meno is just fishing for compliments, or more precisely for being compared with something in turn, Socrates berates him:

– I'm not going to oblige you. And as for myself, he adds, if the stingray paralyses others only through being paralysed itself, then the comparison is just, but not otherwise. It isn't that, knowing the answers myself, I perplex other people. The truth is rather that I infect them also with the perplexity I feel myself.

Virtually Socratic and rascally at the same time, the ray is thinking's quandary, paralysis of speech, an infection at the heart of philosophy.

Scholars seem perplexed by the word itself: how are they to translate Plato's ray? It has them in a spin, as if it were narcolepsy reified, as if in a reality haze, language in drag, drugged, dredging up first one creature then another, out of a dead language a new respiration. It's elementary: the stingray, says one, the electric ray, says another, the torpedo, the flat ray, the numbfish, the narky, the fish that numbs or narcotises.

For Pliny its narcotic qualities were reckoned a cure for headaches, the ray palliatively at play in the migraine. Pliny also knew, and so therefore very probably did Plato himself, that the torpedo ray or narcofish does not numb or paralyse itself. Still in this image of self-numbing there is the strange thought of autoimmunity, a couple of thousand years early. Socrates is the rascally ray, experimentally auto-narcotic. Whatever he may say, the ray remains. It is nature's way, nature awry. Socrates looks like the flat narcofish in the sea, says Meno. (Regarded, at least by some scholars, as a reference to his snubnose, we are thus offered a rare glimpse of Socrates' physical appearance.) And then Socrates is like the ray in relation to what he does to others. He numbs mind and mouth. The ray in Socrates generates aporia. The ray is the figure of the already. It's what Meno knew all along, in an eerie way, the ray of hearsay, the paralysing figuration of all knowledge as recollection.

Ω

Down small familiar country roads I race in the late afternoon sun, finding the store still open and acquiring the relevant items. My father will be pleased, I think, he'll appreciate my having tracked down the very thing, or not, perhaps no. No, this morning for the third time, why the fairytale precision, the cockcrowing fabulous knowing, for the third time in as many days, first over the phone the day before yesterday, then to my face yesterday, and then this morning a third time he said:

– I am beginning to see the attractions of euthanasia.

In the devastating lightnesses of his language, ghost-train supersonic in the airy turquoise gulf, for twenty minutes with a cold beer in a cliff-top garden hanging over the sea I sit wondering at his words. He makes euthanasia sound like a woman, or man, old as the hills. To be exact, this morning he said:

– I have begun to think that there may be advantages to euthanasia.

It's like a pitiless game, euthanasia keeping a step ahead, having a better hand. On the phone and then again yesterday it was word for word the same:

– I am beginning to see the attractions of euthanasia.

Back at the hospital he is asleep but a nurse asks me along to another room to have a chat with the doctor. The doctor tells me she has examined my father and is concerned about his condition.

– Obviously he's feeling not too special, she says, in one of those euphemisms I imagine she reserves for the seriously ill.

She has given him an ECG and discovered his heart rate is twice what it ought to be; no wonder he isn't feeling too special. Also there appear to be some signs of jaundice, she tells me, which could mean, if there is cancer, it has reached his liver, but could mean a variety of other things. It's too early to say for sure: gallstones, for example, can produce a similar effect. But for the moment, she says, she has prescribed something to slow his heart down and hopefully (yes, she uses the word in that hopeless way) make him feel more comfortable. She proposes keeping him in for the weekend and seeing how he is on Monday. He already has an appointment booked for next Friday to have a barium meal x-ray at the main city hospital, some twenty miles away. Cancer has been a suspicion for some time. For the past three or four months, he has complained to me of back pain but has refused to see a doctor about it.

Special beyond speciousness of words: my father has not been to the doctor's, let alone a hospital, in more than thirty years. I try to take positives from this conversation with the doctor: perhaps it is not cancer after all, perhaps it is primarily a heart problem, the medicine she has prescribed will steady him no end, and he'll be feeling much brighter in a day or two. The way a life shifts, paths reconstituted, scopes collide. Another thing, yes, collapsed. The ECG, she says, shows that my father probably had a heart attack about two years ago, around the time, in other words, of my mother's death.

– Silent heart attacks are not uncommon, the doctor explains.

Typical of him to say nothing, I think, to have a heart attack and not even notice. I go back to the ward to find him awake but drowsy. The blind man's wife is now present and the man with learning disabilities has taken his chair out through the french windows and is sitting in the sun. I tell my father about the ECG, the heart attack and steadying medicine. I'm not sure how much he has been told while I was away or how much he understands. Things are becoming so complicated. His face seems difficult of access, like approaching a mountain moving in fog. Yet his eyes are open as a child's. I feel I am the only person in the world who really knows how to address him, how to be heard. And I experience this as something at once always felt and never registered till now.

Words for my father, to and of my dearest funniest Biblical father, dropping away. My beautiful father: tears starting once more to bulge in my eyes, I fight them off, order them back, this madness of lachrymosity. Lachrymimosa, as if I touch with words in my head and they shrink back, military tears standing to attention, veteran characters, starry-eyed, medalling, at a touch transported, bright young things just starting out, awaiting orders, ready to leap. What has made it possible in the past between us, to keep away weeping, all these years, is gone. Because it is going it is gone already. In his esoterically Buddhist way, he has always stressed the joys of silence, the turns of taciturnity. To tire the sun with talking and send him down the sky was never an option. Conversation with my father has always been a minimalist art. And from his eyes in all these years unwitnessed, it now occurs to me, even a tear of sadness shed. Unshed: the mountain of my father's face, seen now going, the haunting cataracts.

Love in a hut become: Innocence, in a shed. My father's shed, the small wooden edifice close to the house, humbly under lock and key, more or less unused now for several years, stuffed with a thousand tools and layered with sawdust, buried worktop, variety of vices, drills, files, knives, holemakers, hammers and chisels and axes and a hundred sandpapers, place of canny retreat. The years roll call back:

– Where's Dad?
– In the shed.

Smallest room not in the house, tears unshed knowing not where. To shed – I shed tears for my father, shed past and present strange word I don't say, only think, his word, his place, separating separated, parting from apart forever a part, to shed, the shed a shade, as if for the eyes, from all other eyes, in the shed sad, shade sad said, where's Dad.

The funniest thing about the shed, the funniest thing about the whole house, the house beside itself, is the electric cable my father set up to run to the shed, at a height of perhaps seven feet, like a miniature telegraph wire, many years ago inadvertently severed by his wielding a ferocious hedge-trimmer, then almost as quickly mended not by replacing the cable but enclosing the damaged section in a transparent plastic bottle, shedding the house, shed or house on a drip-feed. Shedding tears for my father my English shadow, shadow words shadow wards, I, a doll with real tears, take his hand, holding hands, his breathing hard, as if he had permanent hiccups, a hiccius docius, hocus pocus, a struggle aspiring to expel air, right a blockage, surface a summit, or summat, his joky occasional pronunciation of some words, summit like that.

I tell him about the new pyjamas and underwear I managed to buy.

– How long am I going to be here? he asks, as if he hasn't heard anything anyone's said.

– Two or three nights and then we'll see how you are, I say, with luck by Monday you'll be feeling stronger and better.

They're bringing round dinner now, cauliflower cheese followed by custard trifle. Breathlessly in tortoise slow-motion, pausing as if at every other moment to hiccup and every time falling short, he ingests perhaps three half-mouthfuls of the cauliflower cheese, once one of his favourite things to eat, so simple he even knew how to cook it himself. Perhaps three half-mouthfuls, a couple of sips of water, nothing more. I notice there's a radio fixed in the wall above his bed and it's almost news time. At home in recent years he has spent a good deal of time watching TV, dividing the time between 24-hour news programmes and, in the evening, a string of soap operas. I ask him if he'd like to hear the news. He shakes his head:

– There isn't any these days, he says, it's all just terrorism.

I sit with him quietly as he drifts, nods off then wakes, clear-eyed. While he sleeps I try to read one of the books I've brought along to the hospital. I wasn't sure how long I might be here. Then he wakes again. I rest my hand on his. Up starts the theme-tune of the first of the soaps, on a TV that must be in the adjoining room. I decide to see if I can't get a nurse to provide a television for him.

– So that, I tell him, you can watch your soaps.

– No, he says flatly, I don't want to watch them, they're not interesting any more.

Already he's drifting off again, then coming to once more, innocent as a little boy.

– I'm going to go now, I say. I'll be back in the morning around ten and hope you'll be feeling better by then. Have a good night's sleep.

– See you, mate, he gasps, propped up in the bed.

He's held his right hand up in a kind of final salute and gives me a smile, as I make my way out. My father's smile:

he has often said how difficult it is for him. Laughter yes, in the past great waves of laughter, groaning writhing openmouthed, and yes, tears, of course, he would laugh to tears, tears of engulfing comedy. But to round his face up into a full and simple smile he is not able. With the result that there is no midway stopover between a somewhat straining almost sheepish half-smile, ghost or studied intimation of a smile, and at the other extreme a widemouthed beaming bordering on the maniacal. It is to this wavering accompaniment that I depart.

Ω

In the middle of the night the phone rings. It rings and rings, but I don't hear it. The hospital calls. Then the police call.

I get up in the morning oblivious, shower and breakfast, and I feel even faintly upbeat. I managed to get my father into hospital, where he's being properly looked after. Put aside thoughts of the silent heart attack, the disaster of the past, thumping on. The drug prescribed by the doctor will with luck stabilise this and in a day or two he'll be much perkier. The other doctor, the one who came to the house the day before yesterday, surprised but comforted me when he suggested Dad might benefit from taking some antidepressants for a while. Well looked after all might be well.

I picture arriving, my father awake bright-eyed propped up, very glad to see me, and I walk through the main entrance of the hospital quite clear about where I am going, along the corridors down to the ward, making to walk by the desk staffed by nurses on duty, with only the thought of seeing my father in mind. But a woman, with long dark hair, a nurse is standing in front of me, asking would I follow her, back down the corridor. Expressions on other nurses' faces suggest they know who I am, even though I don't recognise them. She opens the door to an office and shows me in. And then the light, there is no light, only so-called natural light suddenly awry. As if it were a magical trick, a party piece: How did you do that? I almost ask aloud. But to whom: the nurse, my eyes, the light itself? The room in absolutely bizarre light, with a couple of chairs, a desk and computer, filing-cabinets with nurses' forenames on different drawers: it is a telegram. Transparency's night letter, stop. Catastrophe of the eye, stop.

I'm not going to tell the nurse not to open her mouth but I imagine, before and after, the unprecedented encounter in this poky little office, a lapidary telegram, as if the light preserved in stone, a miracle. I have never seen anything like it. I could literally cry out, My God! Look at the light! What's happened to the light?

– Sit down, please.

I see from the identity card on her chest that she is called Mary. But it's too late. Everything is so too late. I hear myself saying: We could walk around this, inspect it, dance or run from every angle, stand on the chairs, the desk, crawl inch by inch up the walls, don't speak to me, Mary, I'll never see you again, we know that, you'll never see me or me myself. By requesting I sit down, Mary, you have destroyed the world.

In the event, she doesn't do a fine line in gentleness, something brittle and hard in the voice. My father is dead. Yes I can read, but: they don't know how he died.

She's very tensed up, conscious that this is her duty, the one who has been singled out. (*You* tell him, Mary.) As the senior nurse on duty this morning she braces herself, treading the shaky border between compassionate delivery of the news and adminstrative care to minimise any suggestion of negligence, any possible grounds for litigation.

– I'm sorry to say, she begins, speaking at last, long after the end. I'm sorry to say your father passed away in the night. We tried calling you a number of times, and the police also tried to contact you.

– Oh, I say, oh.

(We've tried to contact you more times than we care to remember: that line, telephoning home and I don't hear.)

– The phone is downstairs, I didn't hear it, I never heard a thing. Did the police phone or did they actually call at the house?

– I believe, she says, they came to the house.

This has to be a lie, I think, or at least highly unlikely, since the front door is directly below my bedroom window and the doorbell is piercingly loud, inside and outside the house. What does it matter, not sure I understand you, you can, can you explain please? Your father fell out of bed in the night, there were no witnesses, the only other people in the room were two gentlemen, one of them is blind and the other has learning disabilities, brackets hanging in silence so neither could give evidence in a court case should you find yourself meditating on the idea of mounting one brackets. A nurse had checked the room only a little while earlier, brackets a silent barrage of questions, as in a game of hangman the gallows steadily rising: a little earlier than what?

19

when? how do you know if you don't know, as you say? earlier than his death, you mean? or his dying? there's a difference, isn't there? brackets, but evidently he fell out of bed and bumped his head, brackets and couldn't get up in the morning that is certainly singsong merrily on high what we are both thinking, brackets. The nurse on duty brackets name not supplied, no night letters for her brackets found him, unfortunately, on the floor, brackets brackets: why were there no brackets attached to the sides of the bed as there often are in hospitals, precisely to ensure that this kind of thing doesn't happen brackets brackets brackets exclamation mark query. Interrogation mark today and from now on, because, how many times does she say this I wonder, is it only once, and couldn't get up in the morning, because there were no witnesses and, does Mary this virgin speaker say *and* or *or*, or if not *or* something like *in any case*:

– There were no witnesses in any case we don't yet know the cause of death. I'm afraid there's going to have to be a post-mortem.

I have no notion when, how or why the nurse leaves me, perhaps it is to inform the police so they know to stop calling me, stop telephoning home, stop calling round, like a herd of storm-troopers, at any rate she leaves me in this night letter slowly stop disintegrating into thundery light stop pointing out the dark green object on the table with the words:

– There's a telephone here. If you want to call anybody, please feel free.

So this is it. I am the winner of some competition, or runner-up, my consolation prize, however long I want to make phone calls courtesy of the National Health

Service to whomsoever I please, no expense spared, no bourn ruled out. He's where? I want to ask. And did the blind man not hear anything? Unable to move I make my way mentally through the door, down the corridor, to the room, and I see the blind man and the gentleman with learning disabilities and there, in the corner, the bed empty, remade already, without the lightest trace of previous occupancy.

Nary Mary quite contrary: call someone, yes. In Tibet for instance, my father always had a fondness for Tibet. Calm caves and mountain monasteries. He never went there, but it's the thought that counts, nary that. Or in Madagascar. Or is it *on*? An island so immense: does anyone say *on* England? Never went to Madagascar either, no matter, all the same, any random number, put me through, chance following the international country code, speak English, no, not a word, nary that, all awry, telephoning home, no, never mind, already impossible, hallo, my father has died, he's gone, given the world the slip, I am sorry I can't linger, Tibet, I haven't phoned Madagascar. So many calls to make, call alarm system that is me, not in, not on, no one dead-end no answer, not a word. I remain, unmoving in my seat.

Ω

To follow this yarn you have to go back into what is called deep time (as if there were any means of doing so). Once upon a slime, before the creation of the Andes, prior to the earliest fossils (naturally, cartilaginously, not a leg to stand on in that department, today any more than of yore), over 220 million years ago, ranged the ray. No yarn without ray: long before the dinosaur, or anything of ragged claw. Anticipatory of the pterodactyl, but how softly, how irenically! And in the sea, the sea itself so strangely kin: for what other creature so accurately mimes or seems already shadowing it, the seeming flatness, swell and roll, the curl and lapping of its wave-wings? In the sea, in the seas, though not ceaselessly. For it came to pass that the Andes were raised up and waterways earlier radiating into the Pacific met up with nowhere to go, the Amazon now reaching into the Atlantic through other hydraulic routes. It was party time. As it became increasingly difficult to juggle life between the Pacific and the brackish or freshwater, as the great sea was gradually, over millions of years, sealed off, the ray developed the capacity to tolerate and finally make itself at home, *chez* the ray, in freshwater. The anal gland ceases to function. There is scarcely any urea in its blood. A ray without urea in its blood and tissues is not one to get in a flap for salty waters. Ray segregation accordingly: freshwater over that side, marine over this. And all of this, keep in mind, took place in what is called deep time (as if there were any other).

Ω

Mary comes back with two green plastic bags with little white name-sticker bracelets on the handles, my father's belongings, and then I leave.

My father's house is the family home of twenty-five years, a cottage dating back to the eighteenth century, situated half a mile or so up a single-track lane, standing in seclusion in an acre of what were once beautifully tended gardens and a small piece of woodland, with fine views of the valley below. In recent years especially, the garden has gone to wilderness. My father managed to cut the lawns in the immediate vicinity of the house, but beyond that the grasses, cow parsley, nettles, brambles have grown above head-height. Even his shed, only a few feet from the house, is inaccessible, with brambles and nettles and the side of a huge hedge overgrown across the door.

I drive back there with surprising calmness. I put the green bags of belongings down just inside the front door. I see someone at the hospital has written on a slip of paper the date, his name, the letters R.I.P. and a list of contents, duly signed:

1 pair slippers
5 pair pants
1 pair pyjamas
1 vest
1 Belt
1 jacket
2 Hankies
2 Jumpers
1 Polo Shirt
1 Pair trousers

Why do some of these words merit capital letters and others not? Did the nurse who wrote them unconsciously suppose, as the text went on, it would be more dignified for these articles to have caps, words cap in hand, begging not to be read too carefully, while also not to be overlooked? As the priest says, we bring nothing into this world and it is certain we take nothing out. Naked and crying we come, in darkness invisible go, leaving two green plastic bags as today's riposte to Egypt's ancient dreams, as if, as if

– I'm sorry, sir, you can't do that.

– Couldn't I at least take my glasses? No one will notice I've got them on, and it'll make such a difference if I can see. (Through the departure gates, not even a boarding pass.)

– No, madam, I don't care if your name is Cleopatra, he's already gone.

– There was something I had to give him.

– That's what they all say. There's always something: a bite for the journey, a few last words, a kiss, a clasp of the hand, iron grip, rip, no, rules is rules. Rip into the world under strict orders, nothing extra out, not a sausage. Try all sorts these days, seen some fine cases I can tell you. It's no good, same as it ever was as far as we're concerned, *Up and down the City Road.* Easy to see why you think you come in, *In and out the Eagle*, but just because you come in doesn't mean, *That's the way the money goes*, pardon me for singing, doesn't mean you actually go *out*, like there is some plane for you to catch, or even any departure gates, *Every time when I come home*, it's a lonely job this, I tell you, most people these days think of us as machines, *I think I'm gonna be sad*, no, in peace we say, daft, the rest likewise, *She's got a ticket to ride*, I says to her I says *ticket*, you don't need no *ticket*, it's all free, completely free, not a bean, I says to her, *But she don't care*, receding hair, wispy silverwhite and gray. Lovely man as a matter of fact: *Pop goes the weasel.*

Ω

Unless that's wrong. Yes, I'm skipping. It's still Saturday. The green bags don't come till I pick them up on the Monday morning.

Now that he has died, I no longer know how long anything takes.

As if on stage, I try to say that minimal palindrome so close to 'dead' perhaps lisped from the start with that skip in view: 'dad'.

I stand in the main room just inside the front door, the dining room we called it, though no one ever dined in it, dining died out before we moved here. I open the door to my left, it's been a habit for two or three years now to keep doors closed in the house, part of his strategy for keeping mice out, or perhaps in, for the strategy has never struck me as very coherent, at any rate to minimise their movement. He has even constructed precisely measured, tried and tested, weighted rods of wood and aluminium for sliding into place once a door is closed, especially last thing at night, having discovered the little creatures can easily scoot under. I walk into the drawing room and draw my breath, absurd to reason, dining and drawing, all these dying words, rooms in tombs, for drawing breath, withdrawing-breath-room. I stare about this large and splendid space, with its oak beams and windows on three sides and fireplace on the fourth. There are armchairs and sofas, tables and sideboards, but most of all there is post. What a word. And now the tears come to my eyes for the first time since it happened, alone:

– These things happen from time to time.

The tears surge like waking up in Eden, in need of Eden. In the wings all this while, yet it was only yesterday they ran down my face as my father lay upstairs in his room, dying it can now be said, dying in neither the dining nor drawing room, can be said *post*, post saying past, all post past past the post. The room is almost knee-deep in junk mail, a choked sea of pointless post. My father never, so far as I know, sent any money to any of these scam-mongers, but he seems also never to have given up believing that somehow some day one of these proclamations that he was winner of the lucky draw, sitting in the lucky drawing room, would come true and a cheque for some huge amount of money arrive in the post. He would receive up to twenty items a day, meticulously open and read them, then replace the letters in their envelopes and annotate the envelopes with a summary of what the senders were promising, the amount of money they wanted from him first of all, the date of receipt, and the deadline for response. In the past six months the mounds have risen dramatically, he stopped bothering to throw the stuff away. But he kept up this barmy archivism, annotating and specifying dates. Now the post is so deep you can hardly cross the room, his armchair the solitary accessible island, humble sedentary fortress lapped by postal tides.

It's Saturday morning, the day of my father's death: he would have wanted details of the date and hour, the precise time. His obsessive love of time, his fascination with the hour meant manual, radio-controlled or atomic, battery or electric, clocks bought by mail order, watches received as so-called free gifts on the waves of junk mail, clocks and watches all over the house, the most accurate and reliable of all of course strapped silver on his wrist, bright bracelet of time as he stood in the kitchen day after day, year after year, at the appointed hour listening to Big Ben or the pips on the radio, checking his watch and commenting on how on or out of time it was. His love led me once, years ago, to the caustic comment that I could imagine his last words, on his deathbed, looking in my eyes and asking:

– What is the time, please?

Ω

The post is past. Words come away. Letters capsize. She is digression, syncopation, asyndeton, ontradiction. Her 'c' curls off invisibly, leaving the shoreline of a new language: *ontra*. She touches all the words, she's amid them, mad as Midas, without a trace. Of course the matter is impossible:

– Everything you write about me, she says, is old and worn out. I am just a character in a book to you.

She is due to arrive this morning, from a great distance. Originally it was the other way round. Reality ontradicts. Because of my father's condition I cancelled my flight:

– He is very weak, I cannot leave him. Will you come to me?

She is pristine. I would like this word to do justice to her, in her absence. I picture this job vacancy, taking a position as an overly well-dressed man who leads people around some local caves, not with a view to telling them about matters of age and rock-formation, what the caves were used for during wartime, how effective they once proved for the cultivation of mushrooms or for clandestine royalist meetings during the civil war or for haunting by a demon lover, but in order to address, soften the audience, explore aloud and without interruption the angelic oddity of *pristine*. Say it, in the dark, to be prised aurally. *Pristine*. Paid by the local tourist board to conduct small groups about in almost pitch-blackness, underground, I am investigating the subject of pristine. Strange well of feeling, curvature of space, unseen the caves except for a single hurricane-lamplight held aloft.

– You might think they know you inside out, I begin. In these caves nothing is what you imagine: everything becomes pristine. Listen. *In these delicate clinkings prised*, I add, with a kind of irritating emphasis.

I need to get their complete attention. Tin lamp on wrist, cavernous prudence, intestinal possession. Enormous difficulty of trapezoid act of speech to get the punters to listen properly. It's a nightmare of a job: rush nothing, slow down to a speed that might just ontradict everything a man or woman has thought, treading carefully in the lamplight. Cold air always the same temperature. Pristine bazaar.

– If I attune my mouth with sufficient precision, and align my ear, I can reveal the names of everyone in this cave, at the drop of a pin, I say to them as a warm-up.

It is necessary to come up with something, after all, and I no longer see the point of saying anything unless it is in the form of a pronouncement made effectively with my dying breath. Many auditors could be forgiven for having already abandoned me, but I have a job to do, in the employ of the local authorities, not a significant salary but I wouldn't be doing this for the money would I, for me it's about supporting a new phenomenon spreading far beyond any cultish local initiative, for the authorities it goes without saying it is also a previously unheard-of tourist money-spinner, how to get grockles, that is the dialect term in this part of the world, how to get them, or the locals themselves, down into the otherwise out-of-bounds and commercially pointless caves and allow them to experience something to set their ears ringing, have them recall and talk about it to family and friends, like so many echoes, long after listening, generating notable future income of ear and pocket.

– What on earth is he talking about? I overhear a disgruntled fellow asking.

That's it, I say to myself, I don't take offence. I request that the gentleman repeat the question and I listen with the special attentiveness that I have acquired from spending innumerable and improbably long hours in the caves and, after a pause, I say simply:

– Your name is Thomas Swarovski.

And the man in question is of course awestruck, as are others in the group, and the problem then is to quieten them down so that the event doesn't turn into an audio-freakshow of clamouring infantilism, what's my name, tell me, tell me, or conversely, for this can also happen, to placate any listener who should then voice their surmise that Thomas is just a plant and I knew his name before we entered the caves. In truth, however, it is an easy thing to do: if you attune your hearing properly in the silence of the caves and listen, most people are speaking a more or less audible version of their name in most of the things they say. It consists in a sort of layered or side-on effect, like the skull in Holbein's *Ambassadors*, a kind of private embassy of the ear, hallucination's jinn.

But in the ordinary run of affairs how many people go out of their way to pass even five or ten minutes in a good deep cave completely cut off from the outside world and take the opportunity to hear themselves speak and really listen to themselves? It can come to seem strange that people pay good money to entertain or instruct themselves with drugs or sex or universities or even submit themselves to psychiatric counselling when they could just as well spend a few free minutes in the silence of an impressively tucked-away cave and experience this ordinary auditory apocalypse, discover themselves as never before. And so, in this foolhardy attempt to unearth something astonishing resonating in the depths of their being, I submit to the group's special attention the word or rather the sound: pristine.

By this point they are of course a divided crowd, some receptive to the angelic oddity, intrigued, even rapt, others who just cannot be doing with it, riled and stirred to opposition by all appearances of magic or conjuration for, as I happily avow, it really is a kind of hocus pocus, of a weird but utterly innocent variety. They won't be going back to tell Jack or Nina about this fiddle-faddle some fellow tried on them in some caves one rainy afternoon when they were at a loose end for something to do away from the beach, or perhaps they will mention the thing but they won't have twigged, they won't have gathered that this, yes, this little outing to the caves is the closest thing they will ever have to an apprehension of what it is to hear oneself and 'be someone'.

And if I were absolutely to clamber up on my soapbox, an obviously ridiculous piece of equipment for a cave, indeed just what the spelean setting ecstatically slides from under you, if I were to ski or be skied in this way, I might go further. I might very readily proclaim that it is here, in the sonic simplicity and purity of these subterranean environs, that it becomes possible to return, yes, for there is always some echo-effect, to return to that conjectural snatch of what it is to be at the very threshold of life, being born, in amniotic oblivion, and in this moment think, and speak.

It is always the speech of a stranger, of course, that is doubtless why Jack and Nina are never any the wiser. In this chamber, in such darkness, by the simple light of this lamp, scrabbling about in your minds for memories of similar experiences or correspondences, from cunts to Plato and beyond, you will understand nothing, no, nothing will come home to roost. But in the blissful disappearance of soapbox merely say pristine, this quaint idiocy almost pretty, almost philistine, almost christian, and none of these but odd, yes, above all in the jets of its pure, clean, fresh, unused, untouched effects, the house, sports field or voice in pristine condition, for example, and in the same breath, as was, formerly, the original, ancient, most olden days and nights, living daylights of night's day. Pristine: fresh and ancient.

– Listen.

Predictable hushed silence. Shuffling of a foot or two, someone vaguely stifles a yawn or cough. Day's work done. At least until the next group. Rarely applause. Group-clapping in a cave is never to be advised: undesirable confusion of amassed bats stirring.

Ω

The ray is stationary. You wouldn't even register it there, retracted into its environs. It sees you before you see it. The ray lies on the substrate. On it, in it, what you will. The ray is prone, adoringly, to a decent bottom. Without an appropriately sandy, muddy or gravelly one, the ray cannot bury itself, which it does both in self-protection and with a view to prey. Vivisepulture is its lifestyle. Now you don't see it, now you do. Then not now again. The ray blends in with the substrate, altering appearance, what is around disappearing into it, eye encrypting camouflage.

All these words, ravaged from scratch.

You say the ray, concerning this solitary surreal tea-tray, this creature of clairvoyant charactery, and all is lost already. The ray is stationary, as if invisible, a nocturnality. You call it *it*, and ditto, lost already.

To say the ray is stationary is to invoke the question of singularity, this solitary ray, straightaway. It is a great problem, shield-shaped, you might suppose. Really, it is enough to put the world in disarray. To bring such a creature to account, to arraign it: that's out with the bathwater in advance, when it comes to the ray. It's categorically different from man or woman. The woman is this one, a writer, for example, not woman, the man this man, a lawyer, say, not man. 'The ray' operates incommensurably. It can be understood generically, as a term for all the rays that ever existed, including the countless millions in deep time, bearing in mind that deep time at once somewhere no one will ever be visiting and, to coin a phrase, the substrate of the present (see above). Or 'the ray' can mean just this or that one, singularly. Language wrecks the ray. Revealingly perhaps, the comparison doesn't hold in the same way in the case of children. The child is closer, in this respect if not in others, to the ray. But the ray is a problem, insuperably so. Or rather, it is an aporia. The ray wrecks language. The revolutionary ray: you reach for words, you riparate. You dream of a new vocabulary, a new reality. Or it dreams you.

Ω

What does a man do on the day his father dies? Outside the sun has taken up the baton for another hot summer day. But the relay has stopped. He wonders if he is capable of driving. He thinks at the time he manages it quite well. Later he will receive a speeding ticket, for driving too fast that morning to collect her from the bus station some twenty miles away. He arrives an hour or so early. He parks close to the station and walks around a crowded Saturday morning country town. Like an altercation developing in his peripheral vision he becomes aware that time has slowed down to a catastrophe. Whatever is occurring is occurring with unbelievable, piece-by-piece, falling-apart diffusing diffracting *lentissimo* decrepitude. No cinema, mental or mainstreet, could capture it, the jostling soundless shopping centre crowds, the lentic swamp, the shattering lens. What he is trying to make out has slowed down to something grinding but imageless, weightless as the noiseless rip of detaching a retina.

And at the same time, in this life-ending slowness, this being a mollusc under someone's descending shoe, he finds himself walking into a clothes store with a

MASSIVE UNBEATABLE SUMMER SALE. Disturbed by his own calmness and foresight, he buys a pair of black trousers and a lightweight black raincoat he can wear to the funeral.

Back at the bus station it is restless, people milling about, dull but strange oppression. He asks does anyone know about the bus from Heathrow. Because it is a Saturday the ticket office is shut. Gradually it emerges that there has been a pile-up on the motorway and the resulting chaos means indefinite delays. He manages to establish that the crash occurred too early for her coach to have been involved. He tries to shrug off the thought that the day is imitating itself. It's something quite alien, he thinks, to that falseness in the impressions of external things that Ruskin called pathetic fallacy. It's as if perception itself were a strange mimosa. Everything seems shadowed, shadowing something else.

It should be hallucinational news.

He sees a man, a blind man, standing at the very edge of the pavement, in danger of stumbling off the kerb or being swept into the air by the next passing bus. He is wearing an intolerably hot, shabby brown winter coat and bearing a sandwich board with the announcement:

SCIENTISTS DISCOVER NEW MIMESIS

This waiting at the bus station is an orchestrated revision of what happened in the hospital, in someone else's mind's eye. He anticipates, open-mouthed, the reappearance of Mary, even darker-eyed than earlier:

– Sorry about this, she says, this sort of thing happens from time to time. You just have to wait for it to pass. It is the aleatory procession, you can never tell how long it is going to last. And when it is over is when it begins. Just wait and see.

It is as if the people who are waiting in vain, either to collect family or friends or to travel themselves, are in truth, unaware, waiting for test results. The gloom of uncoming buses is repeated in the sky. The brilliant sunshine is inexplicably smacked on the back of the head. Big clouds tumble over, clowns without coherence. The darkness spreads like strong, spilt medicine. Gusts of wind scrap, a chill has crept in. Is this his father's work? There is nothing eerie about it, everything is simple and matter-of-fact. He goes back to the car park to put more money in the meter and pick up something warmer to wear. In the back of the car he notices the unbeatable knockdown sale-price black trousers and black raincoat he has bought. The sky looks so black it must open.

Back at the bus station news has filtered through that no one has been injured in the accident, and other bus arrivals have been held up by two to three hours.

When she comes it is as usual as if she had beaten him to it, been hiding round the corner and sprung out like the return of the dead that she always will have appeared.

She sees the blank pall of a man undone. He takes her in his arms. She observes his trembling and waits for his speech. He says, already weeping into her shoulder and neck and ear:

– He's already gone.

It is as if she knew, gathering it thousands of feet in the air, over the night ocean. For some minutes he is fixed, like a piece of paper blown onto her, senselessly secured by the wind. Then he falls back, still speechless. He becomes aware of her baggage, a suitcase and other

35

bags, and wonders how it got there. She tries to take in his stooped, stopped-up form, his strange display of tears in a public place, his frighteningly wiped-out face.

– It was this morning, he says.

On the way home, the sunshine comes back, as if televised, as if the relay were again real, breaking out of a period of implausible interference. Passing through a quiet village, she points out the pretty church and he suggests they stop and have a look. The path up from the lychgate is shady and they pause in the cool of the porch. Her eyes run over the pinned-up notices, her own language but foreign: flower-arranging, organ practice, an announcement for the village fete already two weeks ago. Everything is destroyed. She knows he wants to kiss in the porch, always yes, kiss, the portal, find her lips in the cool shade of the threshold before entering and she lets him, she has him touch her mouth with his fingers, stroke her beautiful face, longing to throw herself into the mirror of his grief while herself already effaced, happy, yes, that she will have been just a character in a book, unrecognisably old and worn away. Nothing of her will get through, not a name, not the faintest vestige of a gesture. She insists on the truth, therefore nothing more can be said. But of course now more than ever with his father dead, she cannot give him up, she cannot leave him. He holds her in his arms in the cool of the porch and runs his fingers through her hair, eyes bulging in stupefied speechlessness gazing into hers, as if she is going to let him be who he had imagined himself being before any of this happened. She lets him kiss her, on the cheeks and lips, she lets her lips be affronted, comforted by the thought that for him she is just a character, she has made that abundantly obvious, and will never be the subject of anyone's attention and all their love-making, so wild and singular and untranslatable, will pass unrecorded.

Ω

The house is inconceivably empty. There is so much to do it seems more logical to leave again, evade the emptiness and perhaps, when the bright day is done, return in the cool of summer dusk. They drive down to the coast and walk up a cliff-path they have taken once before. She feels paralysed. She can only stay a fortnight. In that period she will do everything she can to make things less unbearable. But there is so much to do. He doesn't tell her about the mimosa, fearful of what she would think. The order is impossible to disentangle. There are all things at once. There is the phoning, the labyrinth of calls, family, friends, former work colleagues and of course official bodies, official bodies of death, the hospital to arrange the collection of clothing and other personal items, the doctor to thank her for her help but will he ever make that call, what help, she was so pleasant and clarifying and let him die, the coroner, the man who will actually be carrying out the post-mortem, the people who organise his father's pension, organised, that yawning gap of tenses keeps coming over, gone, no longer to be organised, the bank, the electricity company, the phone company. And then there is the incredible world of the cottage, dead and surviving, stuffed with the past now present, the present now past, in a convulsion of lunatic tranquillity. It's an impossible coincidence, at once a celestial creaking galley, quiet as the moon, and a mine turned upside down with all its shafts, riches and debris suddenly at the surface and no one in charge. No one and nothing is in charge. That's the true madness, as Polonius should have pointed out, had he not been a father himself: the sudden and absolute obliteration of authority. Not that his father was authoritarian, on the contrary he was the least a man could be, but that makes the chasm all the more appalling, into which he now sees he has begun falling. It's not a question of a yes or no regarding this or that thought or desire, this instant of decision or that impulse to act, it's the basis of everything: it's the dissolution of law, truth, rationality, sense, logic, light itself. That's the wizening mimosa, the madness of the truth, seeping into view before the nurse had even told him what had happened, the magisterial, blankety trick-photography of the changing of the light.

Ω

The ray is stationary, lurking in the nether regions. It's nature's way, awry. The sway of nature makes for this singular, this solitary, this ray. There's no getting around it. It's necessarily this one. Irreparably, irrecoverably: it's a ray of one's own. How admirably now each eye is raised, its marvellously wide vision shielded by the lid that, traversing the eyeball as the ray buries itself in the substrate, stops foreign bodies (sand, mud, gravel) entering! Like a spell as yet uncast: *Operculum pupillare!* Even through a glass darkly the ray sees brilliantly, like an underwater cat. In submarine gloom guanine crystals make up tiny mirror-like plates that become visible as the light is fading, just at the outer edge of each eye. How inspirationally it blows and plays, the spiracle or blow-hole behind each eye pumping water like a heart as it lies, almost unrecognisably, on the sandy bottom! On it, in it, what you will. Everything about this brainy creature is so starkly strange, back-to-front and upside down, trapeze artist of deep time, feelings flattened, gravity in chaos. And how charmingly the marine savagery of its eating habits is occluded, since the crafty mouth is concealed, underneath! How readily it would ravage a Red Riding Hood granny, its mouth packed with tooth-plates, arranged in rows! No sooner does a tooth go missing, grinding up its hapless prey, than a new one is lined up in front of it: lifelong self-renewing spray! the original dragon's army! The ray is stationary even when it moves, shooting through water at unnerving speed, propelled by the pectoral fins that form the hem of the body, close to complete circularity, as the axis of the body remains unaltering. How quickly its lurking quivers into larking!

Ω

They have to start somewhere and next day, as if the phone calls are staccato punctuation to a death-sentence uncurling in their ears, they get to work tidying up the downstairs, beginning with the junk mail. Out of order, over the edge, already perhaps too late, he realises there will need to be a reception after the funeral, and then before the reception there will need to be the funeral. It is as if they have lost basic forms of co-ordination, removing or replacing things in the dark, bumping into one another, making love like singed moths. And there cannot be a funeral until there has been a post-mortem.

39

He talks to a voice, in the nearest city, about the body of his father. He has not seen, he will never see the man who performs the post-mortem, the one who sees, but he hears him. As if he might just as readily be talking about the delivery of a washing machine, the pathologist confirms that his father had a knock on the head.

– Which must be due to some fall, the voice concludes (as if he doesn't know anything about what happened in the hospital, as if there was no communication between the two places, as if he would even be required to perform a post-mortem otherwise, the false dog, but)

– In any case, the voice says, this small gash would not account for cause of death.

The cause, the cause. Is it in a good cause, he wants to press, in a counter to all this pathology, to speak of cause of death? To my ear, your very voice is a lost cause, sir. Pause. In which the cause of the pause and the pause of the cause and the pause of the cause of the pause are all in abeyance, without pause or cause, for several days. And then he hears again from this faceless voice with his father's body: the cause of death is two, two causes, and the two causes divide into three, just in case one or two wouldn't suffice, and over the phone they are specified and the words fizzle and faint away, implausible as an electric brae. But they duly reappear, set in the watery strangeness of writing, just a week, less than a little week afterwards, on the death certificate: I. (a) Ischaemic heart disease (b) Coronary artery atheroma; II. Carcinomatosis due to carcinoma of the large bowel.

They collect this from the local register office one bright morning. The blank officious woman taps at her computer, then prints out the incredible document.

Laugh or cry, flick a coin, or watch it melt abruptly in mid-air, it's the hilarity, the nauseatingly absurd handing over of coins, bits of money to acquire more than one copy of the same piece of paper, the death certificate wanted dead or alive. For everyone wants sight of the death certificate, a certified copy, not a photocopy but a certified copy, triggering another chain reaction of phone calls and correspondence: the undertaker, the bank, the pension company, the solicitor's office holding the will, and the vicar to conduct a funeral and the undertaker to liaise with the vicar and the body to be returned to the neighbouring town where his father can, after a week, be viewed in the chapel of rest (When you feel ready, sir), and a time established for the interring and therefore a time for the reception, not wake but reception, like a hotel or motor garage, report to reception, like taking or offering receipt, of what, by whom and how, like nothing. This is to happen at the house, a few minutes' walk up the lane from the churchyard where his father is to be buried in a double grave already assigned alongside his beloved wife dead twenty-eight months earlier.

Ω

The house seems inconceivably full. Every room is a minefield of twilight, never enough light: the dust, the mouse-droppings, the spiderwebs, the sprawl and mounds of junk mail, pipesmoker's paraphernalia, the little stackings and sub-piles, everything collectable collected, the free gifts, the mail order catalogues, the possibly some day reusable envelopes and plastic bags, the phones and TVs, watches and clocks, working or defunct, the habits of collecting keeping storing of a lifetime, the simplest word, a leaf tome. Put them together like chalk and cheese, not in our lifetime even more of a lunacy, as if synapothanumena were bread and butter, the height of fashion, the order and agreement of those that will die together, but life and time in truth never do. They are driving between, in transit perpetually between house and town, starting other collections, starting with all the paraphernalia with which to clean and remove (the cloths and sponges, scouring pads, rubber gloves, cleaning agents, refuse bags), and in transit too between the house and the local tip, day after day the transportation of black rubbish bags, black rubbish bag after black rubbish bag filled with anything and everything judged not to be indispensable. But how is that done?

It is not only the junk mail, which in its mounds is always on the verge of toppling if not toppled into another mound before you can straighten anything out, with all the envelopes that his father has marked as possibles by putting the word 'interesting' and a '?' on the outside of the envelope, together with a date of when the announcement of the prize-winner itself arrived. It is also the presence amid all this junk mail of bills, letters and other documents of significance, bank statements, correspondence with the company that supplies heating-oil to the house, the man who deals with the upkeep of the ride-on mower, letters from himself and from his father's brothers, letters of condolence concerning the death of his wife, the official documentation relating to her death, and then the surfaces such as shelves and mantelpiece piled and bureau-drawers and other cupboards crammed with the entirety of the family's past: photographs and correspondence, but also bits of artwork, bric-a-brac, birthday and anniversary cards, souvenirs, mementos, knick-knacks and other bobs.

Side by side, perched between mounds, they feel their way, murmuring or silent, occasionally seeking advice from one another. Here is a letter congratulating his father on having won fifteen thousand pounds, and another on having won a free holiday to Cyprus, here a bank statement from a year previously and there an invoice for a spare part for the mower. There are notes to himself and letters from others and drafts or copies of letters from himself to others. She is more inclined to jettison, but she also has a sharper eye for sorting potentially significant correspondence or documentation. She maintains the steadier pace, slowly but surely filling the black rubbish bag at her side. For him it is all a haze, she notices, a miasma over his eyes descending with virtually every scrap. Destroy or retain? Why destroy? Why retain? The shores of junk mail lapping at their knees, they proceed envelope by envelope, she the bold pragmatist, he washed over with the impossibilities of decision at the very canuticles of his fingers. And pervading everything all the time, though neither mentions it to the other, is the smell. For her it is curious and alluring, unknown yet connected to him. For him, it recalls the love of life itself, this ceaseless smell of the house. Uncapturable but ubiquitous, on every surface, on every object are the residues, the residutiful, residentical odour that he recognises as not the father's only but that of the house itself. He loves this signature of the house, an olfactory imprint different from anything else in the world, irreproducible and irreplaceable. He dreams of preserving it, bottling and selling it back to himself, privately, on a demented black-market of grief. In reality this smell, neither stench nor perfume, enveloping every object in the room, every item of their clothing, every inch of their hair and skin, endures scarcely longer than the time it takes to transport a car-load of rubbish bags to the tip.

They drive to the tip more times than they can think. In the unrelenting blazing heat of these uncountable, unaccountable days they drive to this place manned by whom or what? These men, what are they called, the workers at the municipal tip? His mother knew the name, he recalled, she would drop it into her conversation as something to be enjoyed by itself, like a mint. But it keeps defeating him, this word, never in his vicinity, repeatedly eluding him, as if with a mind of its own. Then finally, out of the heat and haze, like a little oasis in a mirage it shimmers into focus: the totter. He is the figure who attends a dump, who deals with refuse, the rag-and-bone man of the heart who tots, to totter the word, the tot to tot, to turn to itself, backwards and forwards, a stumbling, stuttering figure of refusal. There are two of them, in fact, every day one or the other and often both, always the same. One of them is a small frightening man, with vacuum eyes looking through your face as if nothing you could say or ask could ever register on his, as if your face were indeed already reduced to bone. They think of asking: Where do we put something like this old Swedish orthopaedic kneeling chair (bought from some mail order catalogue twenty-five or thirty years ago, unsat upon for all but two months of that time), made of steel and deckchair-style fabric? Does it go to metal recycling, or is it general household waste? But they know better. They learn very early on not to ask the tiny totter anything. One false move and he'll melt your face off with a nice canister of stuff fit for purpose kept close in one of his numerous pockets, is how he makes them feel. But the other, oh yes, the other totter! What a brave and magnificent specimen, a totter to tot, a totter to take home to your parents and present saying: Look, I have never known whether I was gay or straight or what it meant to have a sexual identity, besides a fiction out now, as the hoax played day and night by the contemporary universal film company, but this man is a totter, folks! Just check him out – the height of the fellow, the flowing golden mane of hair, the stupendous beautiful dirtiness, mom, your tottering colossus roaming the refuse, the mounds, the tipping-effect, like a god to whom you could address any question, no matter how naïve or obvious, and he would tell you graciously, with simple but unfathomable courtesy, as if completely in your own shoes and in another world at the same time.

How to gauge this disappearance of themselves every time they ask the totter a question? In due course, after a dozen or so visits, they are both in love with him. He is a dreamy but inextinguishable part of their cryptic, shared biography. They pack the odoriferous refuse bags, having separated the rubbish into what can and cannot be recycled, and drive to the tip frankly yearning for a sight of this man, and find themselves deflated, absurdly down-at-mouth on leaving, on any occasion when he isn't there (or is concealed in the totter's marvellously mysterious hut, on a tea or lunch break), as if the tip were another home, a home-making possible thanks to

45

the lion-man who doubtless quit the premises everyday at sundown or earlier but seemed nevertheless to be the very premise of the premises, the king they would like to have invited back to the house, wined and dined, twinned and dazzled, sinned and binned, idylled and idded in an impossible fantasy loved as no one had evidently ever loved him.

Ω

And all the while gnawing, denying nothing everything, in at the entrails parsing and combining, nibbling and morselling, filling black bags in the summer heat, stacking them in the car, driving them down to the tip, hour after hour, things for nobody, breaking off for lunch then back to filling black bags, hour after hour, in order to turn the downstairs into a space that could reasonably accommodate thirty or forty people on the day of the funeral, in the midst of cleaning and clearing always the phone calls, the practical arrangements, the line of authorities and officials stretching out to doom in a hall of cracked mirrors. After the post-mortem it is necessary to set up the date of the funeral and arrange what kind of burial, what kind of service, what time of day, presided over by whom, and on what terms. The vicar who, over the phone, was agreeable to doing it, seems outwardly at ease when she comes to the house to meet the bereaved son and his friend, the beautiful totter-grieving girl, and talk to him about the arrangements, but becomes less comfortable with every passing second, inwardly no doubt from the beginning unsure of just how Christian this burial is going to be. Always a little tricky, so often these days, a problem to combine sympathy with the bereaved with the sneaking sense that these people are not church-going, these people want a so-called Christian burial not on account of their own faith nor even of the faith of the one to be buried, but merely on account of what to call it, I'm flummoxed now, I always get flummoxed at this point, best not analyse it, an aesthetic question really, a matter of appearances after all. Me too, I suppose, the way I drive up to the door and ring and introduce myself as the local vicar, the character who has never met this chap let alone his father but is, within two minutes of getting inside the front door, referring to the dead person by the affectionate diminutive version of his first name, as if I've been a family friend for decades. (Or as if he is still alive sitting in the next room patiently filling his pipe with rhododendron leaves, for that was what he had discovered in recent months he most enjoyed smoking, and the easiest thing to do, fetch a few leaves from the rhododendron bush just outside the front door and dry them out on a plate on the little table next to him.) And as I am standing here discussing the funeral arrangements, what he would like, what he wouldn't, what he would or wouldn't because his wife would or wouldn't have wanted ('like' for the man unburied, 'want' for the woman in the ground, subtle but valid distinctions, in my book), because it's a double grave after all, lest we forget, it's your mum's wishes too, there is something about the way the chap holds back, doesn't speak when I would expect him to speak, something about the other person, where does she come from?

– Are you family, my dear?

– No, I'm not, the girl replies.

47

So who is she? Not going to get a satisfactory answer there either. Something about the man wavering over the standard deals we offer, service in the church or service at the grave.

– Will it be a big event? Many coming? Was your father well known locally? I expect he had a lot of friends.

And the son feels impelled to inform her that his father was a Buddhist who practised no recognisable form of Buddhism, unless you count smoking rhododendron leaves, and his mother was an atheist of the sublime party, and then to complain about the apparent impossibility of setting up a decent burial in this God-bemobbled country, if she'll excuse his language, unless it is a good Christian burial conducted by a bona fide priest such as he takes her to be, and the vicar feels impelled to ensure that she is not dealing here with some strange species of satanist, for there is after all just a flicker of doubt in her bones, she won't call it by name but the chap's chemicals are sending out warning signals. Proceed with caution. Consign to unconscious exorcism.

And the son would like to point out that 'satan' is a rich and beautiful word that indeed need not be invested with a capital letter but can be understood in a sense cut free, if he may put it this way, from all religiosity, as a noun in its older or, perhaps, more pristine sense meaning simply an adversary, someone who opposes or plots against. Not forgetting also of course that the word has been used of some of the funniest characters in literature. Think of Falstaff, that old white-bearded satan.

But she wants to know now what extracts from the Bible and what hymns his father liked, if there is anything special the son wishes to have in the service. Otherwise she'll be happy to suggest something.

Yes, the bog-standard programme, he thinks, with the lord as my shepherd and an excerpt from Revelation he almost starts reciting to her on the spot, And I took the little scroll from the hand of the angel, and did eat it; and it was in my mouth sweet as honey; and when I ate it my belly was embittered; no, don't wind the woman up, she's only doing her job.

So he is havering, yes, she can tell there is something not to be trusted about the bereaved man.

– I'd like to be able to think about this and perhaps suggest a passage or two, perhaps read a poem and say a few words of my own if that is OK, he says.

– Yes, she says hesitating, that would be perfectly all right, so long as it is in keeping with the occasion.

And as for in the church or at the graveside, he says quite firmly:

– By the graveside.

But later he phones her and changes this, having considered the possibility of rain and elderly or less able mourners obliged to stand at length in the graveyard, and would the sound carry, he wonders, in the event of a hymn or reading 'in keeping with the occasion'? What would be the point of it if no one can hear anything?

In the event the rain holds off and they proceed to the side of the double grave standing in grass unmown for weeks, following his reading of Blake's 'Jerusalem' inside the church, he repeating in himself, to the syllable, the as if satirically stern, always surprising force of his father's rendition, its loudness so much at variance with his diurnal taciturnity, a storming on the heights as at school carol services when the son was a boy, blindly cherubic with unbroken voice blushing in a sea of voices, buoyed up by his father's among them.

Ω

Then there is the vicar and the frog. At the omega of her call, at the denouement of what is to be the vicar's first and last visit, all pleasantries ending, without quite going so far as to say lovely to meet you look forward to seeing you at the funeral, he opens the front door, there's plenty of space for her to pass through, but then she retracts more fully the porch door already sufficiently ajar, and he detects a slight sound absolutely out of place, a faint crunch. She hears or seems to hear nothing, evidently too busy in the world of her own virtuous thoughts and feelings, or thinking about lunch, but he knows he hears something. Only after she has driven away does he look down and see in the jamb, close by the rusty hinge, a frog, or what remains of a frog, with possibly a final throe, the throe as he goes to touch, no, not a throe, a cast of the light, a fantastical last contraction. The vicar killed the frog as she was leaving.

What is the frog's place in the yarn? What is this leap of faith into the door jamb and wait for the final crunch, as if that frog is indeed another forgery, a hopping mad music or rhythmic throe, like slime, like a caul, over eyes and ears, like the rhapsody of sky and shadows at the bus station or the feeling of being a mollusc under someone's descending shoe?

And all the while leaping backwards, in an analepsis of ranarian lucidity, through the entire entraining of funeral arrangements and making the downstairs of the house clean and tidy enough to accommodate the reception after the service, at every turn and totting up of post-mortem preparations the bereaved man and the girl-stranger are, merely on his say-so, his implacable, irrefutable position on the topic having become evident to her over a series of evenings following her arrival, his laying out of the design, the vision he has, in order to do what has to be done, on his insistence they are at the same time making way for an impressively large aquarium, to be installed in the dining room. It needs to be longer than it is high, four by two metres and just sixty centimetres deep, the desirability of a pool as large as possible scarcely requiring specification, not only from an aesthetic point of view but in practical terms: if one of the creatures should die, it has far less effect in a large space. Inevitably, in the case of a small aquarium, products of decay from a decomposing body contaminate the water and can rapidly bring about the death of other creatures, but if you think big, if you reckon on the worst with a big showcase space, you can have one be dead and decaying for twenty-four hours or more and it have no unduly adverse effect on the life of the other inhabitants.

These are not his words but she extrapolates them, in ironic form, from what he tells her.

Not to mention the possibility of an electrical fault, say a heater or pump breaks down, and you don't notice because it happens in the middle of the night, or you go away for the day, and come back to find the calamitous aftermath of power failure: with a large aquarium everything is more survivable, changes in temperature or pH level more gradual, salvation is plausible and no creature need die.

– What creatures? And how many are we talking about here? she not surprisingly wants to know.

– Four, he replies, South American freshwater stingrays: *Potamotrygon motoro*.

There is no certainty as to which variant of the type. They might come from Peru, Brazil or Colombia. Many of these species remain unnamed, even undescribed in the scientific literature, but they are distinctive for the beautiful eyespots on their backs, like leopards, peacocks, chameleons or butterflies, and their bellies white as ghosts. He shows her some photographs.

– I've already ordered them, he says.

They are due to be collected on the eve of the funeral and, as if for children to be adopted and brought home to a house where nothing is prepared, with winter coming and no wood chopped or food laid up, they must work like demons to ensure a welcoming environment.

Sometimes he says they, sometimes we, he says things, she notices, that fray or slide off at the edges, splashes of grief paint, verbal splay, semantic bubbles, mimosaturated existence popping before you can adjust your vision to see inside. In the evenings when there is nothing to do besides sit in exhaustion, dusty fusty musty in the twilight of the increasingly empty drawing room, dining room or kitchen, or outside on the garden bench to no sound besides sheep in the field above the house and a washing vaguely up of distant traffic on the road running like an unseen wound along the valley below, they discuss at great length the materials required to be ordered or purchased the following day. Gradually they clear and clean, emptying the dining room sufficiently to paint it.

– We are getting ready for them, he says laughing, slapping it on.

She is surprised at how many of the materials are available locally or at short notice from elsewhere, and at his passion to have the thing done, the rigour of his researches and enquiries, the forays to builder's merchants and aquarium shops in nearby towns, sea-life centres strung along the coast, online companies for aquaculture supplies and aquarium systems.

– I never dreamed we'd custom-build a ray pool, did you?

He makes her face light up with laughter. He works out the volume in cubic inches, divides by 231 to establish how many gallons of water: 2,078. He insists on making the thing out of acrylic, not glass, despite the drawbacks. Acrylic sheets are more easily scratched but they don't crack or break so easily and, in any case, it's much simpler to drill acrylic. When it comes to installing an individual filtration system the last thing anyone wants are dead-spot areas of water. Lack of circulation means anaerobic conditions. The spillway design is likewise crucial. We need to make sure there are appropriate corner overflows to take away the protein waste that tends to collect at the surface. Despite the fact that acrylic constructions come with a significant lip to help prevent any creature escaping, we really need a covering. Of this last he explains:

– No problem. I'll just cut it from egg-crate plastic.

Putting together the frame he shows an expertise and dexterity she has not anticipated in him, forcefully snapping together, securing, screwing, drilling the construction of the stand, taking care to ensure sufficient space inside to enable work on the filter as and when required, tilting and adjusting and finally firmly bedding down the acrylic plates. It makes her laugh at least once a day with an absolutely unexpected pleasure, as if this were really how to live, what to do.

Ω

And then everything is ready, as if fairies have been in labour, the day breaks, the downstairs of the house is clear, everything that needed to go to the tip has gone, everything that could be put out of sight in this or that cupboard has been put out of sight, the drawing room and dining room and kitchen and downstairs toilet have been cleaned and vacuumed and scoured and washed. The dining room in particular has been especially arrayed for the occasion, the table moved off into one corner, the candles, cups and saucers, glasses, plates and napkins set forth, the wine, soft drinks and food all in preparation. Everyone who could reasonably be expected to have wanted to know knows this is the day, the church at two o'clock, friends of his parents and family arriving from far and near. He has written his speech and the two of them are ready, he dressed in the black clothes he bought on the morning of the death and she in black picked up on a later outing to the town. They stand clasping one another in the dining room clad in black amazed at what it seems they have done, disbelieving, as if supernatural forces or forgeries must have been at work; it is time to walk down to the church.

Ω

They have no black shoes. They have been aware of this for some days but failed to take action. Their shoes by chance are green, and this is the first thing the undertaker and pallbearers notice, by the hearse outside the lychgate, some twenty minutes before the official start of the proceedings. The undertaker shakes the hand of each in turn and looks them in the face, but his primary focus is the shoes. His gaze drops to the ground, bright green trainers, both of them wearing green trainers: what is this about, why for the life of him hasn't the gentleman got black shoes and the lady for that matter, the sylph-like slip of a girl who must be half his age? What does it mean, this green, this dividing of green shoes among the two of them? It's a conspiracy, a sign, something not right.

It's a hot day and the undertaker is sweaty already, a corpulent man liable to feel the heat even without all his clobber on, and whether it is the sun or something about the couple, he is not one to be fazed in the course of things, but he is having trouble with these green shoes on the both of them. And what is their relation in any event? Is she his daughter? No, that can't be right, nor his sister, no resemblance there either. And those green shoes in which they are conjoined, up to what could an undertaker like himself ever suppose to be other than no good! What a colour! He'll tell his wife, even more than himself massively overweight, dying off the fat of the land, he'll regale her with the details tonight. After the second funeral and the forty-mile round trip, that evening back in the flat over the funeral parlour, upstairs from the chapel of rest where the son had gone just the day before with the same girl, the wife saw them then, remember, the son come in to pay his respects and the young woman followed like a cat. He never thought anything of it at the time, regarding what their relation was, but the gentleman come in and the undertaker conducted him through to the chapel, a surreal little living room with no television or other furnishings of the living but a chintzy wallpaper with no windows besides one curtained-off interior window that would, were the curtain drawn back, give view onto the stuffy little corridor. It resembled a retro-room in a shabby provincial museum, how life looked decades ago, or so the son thought. Reproductions of landscape paintings are pinned to the walls, lepidopterously; there is a little table with artificial flowers and a faded doily; and *crème de la crème*, you look up to see a little picture of Jesus, the crucial accoutrement to the designation of chapel of rest. What else?

Anything else?

Yes, of course, no twitching at the curtain of the interior window needed to catch that. It is the labyrinth at the centre, the bier or bed or bearing point of life. The day before the funeral and this is the one and only opportunity to see his father reposing, almost prostrate, laid almost horizontally but with a slight propping up of the upper body, the shoulders and head just as he had been last time 'in life'. All our yesterdays a fortnight of solemnity. Day fought to death, seems only yesterday, but then propped up perhaps a shade more, and smiling that faintly Mona Lisa cryptic valediction about which he will never tell anyone unless in a touch, a certain squeeze of the hand, and now so strangeways, all awry, all away, utterly not. As she said when he invited her to come in and stand a moment with him:

– That is not your father.

You expect to see the one who has died, instead this bier, this base, this resting-place empty but for this untenable tenant, intolerable not least because all the time you are acutely aware that the laying out and propping up is but the exhibition of a moment and no sooner will you have vacated the office at the front of the funeral parlour than your lumbering undertaker with the help of his brother-in-law will be carting that one out and bringing in the next for some other's viewing an hour hereafter, and the body not the body but gone away, imprisoned without weight, the air heavy with lilies, the strange starched white shirt sported by the corpse not his father, his face drawn, yes, hollowed away and weirder than waxwork, with eyelids sealed and stitching too on the forehead, a word he always hears in his father's voice, the suppressed aitch introducing a sort of naval charm, familiar as a fo'c'sle, for'ead with the proper dropping of the aitch pronounced deep in a forest of id, not head, stitching not only of the surrounding of the face but for the gash, the foregashed forehead a couple of centimetres long, the trace of the wound sustained when he fell from the hospital bed, unattended and unnoticed for who knows how long, onto something he imagines sharp as gravel.

Ω

So digging into that steak and potatoes his wife cooks that night the undertaker will remark on the son of the bereaved and the slip of a girl with him both wearing spring-green shoes and what is the meaning, in a lifetime of working on the sward, turfing up and turfing back down, he never asked himself about green as such and now with this strange couple it is written all over the churchyard. The vicar arrives and they exchange a few practical and time-of-day remarks, suitably subdued. Neither says anything about being ill-at-ease with the manner of the man and the woman in green shoes, but both are troubled, the undertaker now in particular, by suspicions of superstition, a supernaturalistic greenery jarring with the homely Christian calling that goes with the territory, as of grace omitted before the steak. There's a lifetime's mistaking brought up in a moment like this, spotting the green shoes and wondering quite out of church bounds, and it's a blessed relief he considers, as the pallbearers maintain their shuffles of conversation looking at the ground, that he can keep his thoughts to himself and imagine the place where it's already not possible, what with all the newfangled technology, a man's privacy approaching the verge of extinction.

Ω

The church, once they're all ensconced (besides a cousin who is stuck in traffic and only makes it to the reception shortly before everyone leaves), is cool and surprisingly calm out of the August mid-afternoon heat. There are more people than the son had suspected or could even recognise. Presiding over the proceedings, the vicar has comfortably internalised a *modus vivendi* for dealing with this slightly odd occasion: the bereaved man, evidently not a church-goer, wants nonetheless to read a speech. Complacently she introduces this, after repeatedly invoking in first-name terms the dead man she has never met. In lucid and collected fashion, determined to remain straightforward, neat and audible, he proffers a few remarks about his father's love of words, his gifts with language, his extraordinary precision with syntax, grammar and spelling (he had worked as an editor and proof-reader over many years), and also about his father's passion and inventiveness with things, his skill as a maker of objects and contraptions sometimes more Heath Robinsonian than others might tolerate let alone admire. The speech then moves on to a truncated version of an anecdote about the church in which they are standing, concerning a period around twenty years earlier, when the vicar had no connection with the parish.

One day a builder came and erected scaffolding around the lychgate, presumably with the intention of painting or reroofing or otherwise repairing it, but no one ever followed it up, the days passed and the weeks and months and no one came and no one seemed to mind, besides the son who saw it as a daily eyesore and defacement of the church. Eventually he took it upon himself to type out a statement on the subject, on a single sheet of paper:

THE SCAFFOLDING

One of the most recent and most striking features of the village church is the scaffolding at the lychgate. It has now been in place for a year – some say even longer – and its purpose is shrouded in obscurity. It seems likely that the original purpose of the scaffolding was to facilitate the application of a new coat of paint. Perhaps a more fundamental, strenuous and time-consuming operation had been envisaged: structural repairs to the lychgate? Rumours have been rife. One account which appears to retain credibility locally is the postulation of an argument between a painter and a builder and their consequent parting of ways. The painter may never return; or, of course, may never have existed. Already it is so long ago that few locals can easily picture the church without its parergonal complement. Another rumour has concerned the establishment of a small group known as the village Revolutionary Council, working for the peaceful overthrow of the scaffolding, as well (it is claimed) as the removal of the grotesque bow of barbed wire which secures the little 'kissing gate' round at the back of the church.

Is the scaffolding now a permanent feature at last, a monument in its own right? And if so, should it be attributed symbolic significance? These are questions which, over the past three months in particular, have caused fierce debate in certain areas of the parish. Suffice to bring to notice the philological endeavours of one local historian who has noted the word 'scaffolding' as etymologically of obscure origin but nevertheless as bearing the less widely known sense of 'a raised framework, as for hunters, or among some primitive peoples for disposal of the dead' (*Chambers*). Given the etymology of 'lychgate' (Ger. *Leiche*, corpse), the notion of an alteration in church policy, with regard to the practice of excarnation, irresistibly suggests itself.

This document was signed 'For the people of the village' and dated 'June 1986'. His father apparently delighted in this so much that he created a specially carved wooden platter, like the sort of distended table-tennis bat you find in certain churches with information about the history and architecture of the building. The dead man screwed down this little text about 'THE SCAFFOLDING' under a carefully cut plastic plinth. The son placed the platter in the church that afternoon. Within days the scaffolding was dismantled. Unread at the funeral, this text is nonetheless exactly as the vicar pictured. Every word conforms to her sense of the inside narrative of the occasion.

Ω

He concludes with a few lines from Blake's 'Jerusalem', read not sung, tacitly countering the more obvious option (favoured by the vicar) of everyone singing it in the service, hearing it regurgitated on the cranky church organ, accompanied by fifty or sixty people who cannot sing to save their lives, when the only rendition he wants to hear is the school carol service no one but he can now recall, with his father so improbably but majestically booming out above all other voices: I will not cease from mental fight, / Nor shall my sword sleep in my hand / Till we have built Jerusalem / In England's green and pleasant land. And when he takes his seat again, in the pew at the front of the church beside the pristine girl, her body lightly touching him like a prehistoric egg, still warm, she is contemplating the text about the scaffolding, which he showed her just last night, the platter retrieved from one of the cupboards near the back door stuffed with disintegrating early twentieth-century india paper volumes of the *Encyclopaedia Britannica*.

Excarnation is literature. Its music strips you. Literature is excarnation.

Thinking at death is shared in music. Cut, stripped, loosened, shred, ripped and divided in raving madness. It is waiting everywhere, a word or phrase in a beloved voice, songs, refrains or intonations, symphonies or snatches without identifiable composer or musician, a bar, a melody, permanently interrupted, gone forever, Hubert Parry's Blake and his father's 'Pop Goes the Weasel', Bach's second violin concerto caught in a Sunday evening ribbon of reminiscence flowing through his father's ears, as the church sheds them and they file out towards the spot where his mother's body was lowered just twenty-eight months earlier.

The couple in green shoes are exhausted. It has been the longest fortnight of their lives.

After the graveside blessing, people are to gather, if they wish, to look at the flowers sent from America, France and elsewhere. Time passes.

These things happen from time to time.

Politely but with an unmistakable hint of impatience, the undertaker asks:

– Would you move on away from the flowers now, sir?

You don't stand gawking at the flowers on the grave beyond a fixed period. There's other people would perhaps like to see them, sir, you set an example now, move away and everyone will know to follow, and we can all get on with the business of proceeding out of the churchyard. But for what reason, not only the beauty of the flowers and the afternoon and the breeze and earth and summer sunshine, his father and mother now for the first time together again in name and body consigned?

Already people have begun to vacate the churchyard, however, and he needs to inform them of the reception. Some know already but others have not heard and he wants everyone to understand that they are indeed welcome. Exhaustedly dipping and stepping around gravestones, he tries to pick up on individuals or couples he doesn't know or hasn't expected to see at the funeral:

– Hello, I'm not sure we've met, please come to the house for a drink.

It is a ten-minute walk up the single-track lane. Parking outside the house being difficult, many go on foot. The churchyard resembles a theatre emptying of spectators. The vicar proffers her blandly earnest thank you but no thank you, and the undertaker also gives his excuses, another funeral to attend, a further nigh-on forty miles to drive that afternoon. Only the gravediggers remain. And the man in grief is struck, as with a spade to head or legs, by the scarcely concealed relief of a gathering never to be reconstituted regarding a departure that has perhaps not begun.

Part Two

The reception is for her a treacherous experience of meeting many people for the first time, trying to keep one name or face apart from the next, as a stranger to the house and yet more affected by it now than anyone perhaps besides the son. She is the pristine remora, paradise-haunter, tip-haulage expert, bleacher and scrubber. She is also, this afternoon, chief tea-maker and sommelier of wine, at least until others offer to assist, while the son is still busied with taxiing folk up from the church and overseeing the arrangement of parking. Some people are too nervous to address a word to her, others dutifully say hello and ask where she comes from and what her plans are. She is staying a couple more days, she explains, then must return to her own country.

With so many strange friends and relations the event is at first, not surprisingly, muted. She pictures a specialist section in a music-store, a selection of soundtracks from funeral receptions from different countries, the English version impressive for the quietness of its opening. Bodies shuffle. Some file through to the kitchen, others contend with the dining room. No one can stand in the centre. Voices operate at little more than whispers, amid clinks of teacups and teaspoons, and a furtive crunching of biscuit. But as the scene progresses, it attains a kind of macabre raucousness, rising to crescendos absurdly at odds with the way it began.

And for him the only thing is to let all the visitors see the pool, hardly difficult as it engulfs almost the entire space of the first room you enter as you come into the house. The surprise on some people's faces seems diplomatically slight. With others the intake of breath is audible. Of course he misses so much of this initial impact because he is busy with sorting out parking in the drive and taxiing people up the lane, but the sheer size and scale of the equipment alone is evidently a cause for amazement. The aquarium fits into the oak-beamed room with space for a comfortable walkway around, with access to kitchen and drawing room as well as into the stairwell to the upper floor. The table with drinks and food has been set up in the one doorless corner. It is possible to hold a cup and saucer of tea or coffee or a glass of wine close to you and someone else pass without too much inconvenience, but still for at least a handful of guests it must be difficult not to sense that the gangways around the pool are like the space in the earth around a coffin.

– Well I never, just look at the scale of the thing!

– Did you know he was interested in aquaculture?

It's bigger than the sort of pond children might dream of having in their garden.

– What's in it anyhow?

– Looks like a couple of big rocks and a load of white gravel.

68

– Is there something in it?

– He's taking after his father, wouldn't you say? His dad always was making things and installing them somewhere or other.

– Like something out of Heath Robinson, to be sure.

– Used to drive his dear old wife round the twist, with that filtering system he set up for the drinking water supply. You've seen that, haven't you? Take a stroll into the kitchen and have a look, it's still there. Lord knows how many filters and containers he used to purify the water come from a spring in the field above the house.

– Very father like son, wouldn't you say?

– Only look at the size of it!

– Are there fish in it?

– What's this all about?

Gradually his own voice takes up a place in the room and attention is more sharply focused on the remarkable tank.

– No, it's not empty. They are rays, the son explains. There are four of them. They are *Potamotrygon motoro* freshwater stingrays, from South America.

His aunt is at him, his mother's youngest sister, accusing him of being mad as a hatter. He is smiling, speaking quietly, but everyone is listening now.

– You used to have an aquarium yourself, he reminds his aunt. Though I admit *this* is something of a departure.

– Freaky if you ask me, says the aunt, not one to mince her words, and mildly guilty too at the recollection of her own late husband's insistence on keeping aquarium fish and the palaver of feeding them and cleaning out the water, ensuring the light is kept on for specific periods to eliminate the growth of algae and so on.

– It's a lot of work, young man (an irony this, since he is in truth no longer young, and every day since his father's death has felt like a month and more). How are you going to manage it? I assumed you were going to be selling the house. You can't sell it with a great tank like this *kerplomp* in the middle of it.

The rays, it seems, divide the company like goats and sheep. For some the sight of these creatures, especially when the son opens up a section of the lid and they come truly flap-slapping up to the surface, all too evidently eyeing the wine-sipping peanut-crunching crowd, is just too weird. A wave, or to be more exact, a cold current of strangeness passes through the audience, as if in collective registration of an extravagancy out of keeping with mourning, beyond any normality one might reasonably associate with a funeral reception, a kind of crazy ensnarement, yes, an unacceptable, improper spectacle best reacted to by the quickest practicable exit, but a wave that, the girl senses, once gone gives way to more diffuse and diverse predicaments of being stranded and uncertain. No one, in fact, leaves. And then there are others, it becomes clear, who are simply in awe, astonished at what the son has done.

– Not only me, he says to a murmur along the line of all those gathering around the pool: I could not have done it without *her*.

He gestures towards the pristine dark girl by the door off to the kitchen.

– It is necessary, he goes on, to confront a ghastly deception. Triumph is a terrible delusion that must nonetheless be reckoned with. To pretend that it is not there would be as nauseating as to accept that it is. I cannot speak for her (and here he gestures once again towards the beautiful stranger scarcely anyone present has previously met), but I am not going to deny a sense of achievement at having conceived and constructed this ray pool, with its spillway design and lipped feature, at having lined it with the correct quartz sand, after picking over and assessing it, stone by stone, day after day, at having carefully selected the, I think it's thirteen, individual, perfectly sized rocks, and at having installed the highest-quality filters, pumps, lighting and heating. Everything has been done here that could have been done to ensure an appropriate supply of water and to establish the correct mechanisms for the upkeep and replacing of water, and for the weekly gravel-cleaning and hydro-vac. But any feeling of triumph here is at once also its opposite. To achieve is to lose. To suppose that you are winning is to be undergoing absolute defeat.

He pauses, somewhat perplexed at where this speech has come from. Then he carries on with a view to relating as briefly as possible the acquisition of the rays themselves, the initial quandary he had been thrown into by the dealer who encouraged him to buy a number of so-called teacup rays.

At which point at least one local woman, a farmer's wife, glances down in fuzzy consternation at the teacup and saucer in her hands.

– The teacup ray, the bereaved man adds, as if picking up the demur, is sometimes advertised as a sort of miniature version as of some pigmy species, but really it is just a baby. Don't be fooled by the teacup talk. I wasn't, for I had read and talked to plenty of people on these issues, and I wasn't going to be fobbed off from my original desire to get *motoro* rays of fair proportions which, as you may be able to see, is what we did eventually manage to do. Not that they are as big as they might be: a stingray of this variety can, in appropriate conditions, grow to a diameter of three feet or more, but these I hope will be happy to stay closer to the size they are now.

– It's been hard, he goes on, unexpectedly swallowing a word or two, more emotional now than he had been in presenting his speech at the church, not having anticipated that he would make any particular speech at all at this point, in this revolutionised dining room, in the presence of so many family and friends, as well as a handful of more or less complete strangers.

– It was hard, especially at the end, a matter of such precarious hope – as any of you will know who may ever have bought and kept rays... I don't know, is there anyone here?

And he looks up, surprised at his own question, to a tide of blank faces.

– Perhaps not. But the trickiest part is bringing a ray home in its transport basin. You have to give it time to acclimatise to the change in water, introducing the creature to its new environment with all the care in the world not only for its own wellbeing but also for your own, since these, after all, *are* dangerous creatures. It is usual to cover the ray's sting with a piece of plastic piping during transport, but at the other end, I mean back here at the pool, it was then a matter of removing the plastic hose from each. Not to do so is to invite infection, but to do so is at least as hazardous to the handler as to the ray itself. It was, I confess, a slightly hair-raising operation and I couldn't have done it alone. So far, at any rate, it would seem to have been effective, but naturally it should be stressed (as the speaker now notices one of his cousin's youngest children, a boy of perhaps seven, wander up to the edge of the pool and try to peer in), I should have stressed at the very beginning that these beautiful creatures can also be very dangerous, and when you lift up a section of the lid, as I have just done, and they come to the surface like a club of old wraiths having been stirred by some unexpected knock at the door, don't for one moment suppose that it would be safe to put your hand in and give them an affectionate stroke (the cousin now calling the boy away from the edge) as you might have considered doing if you'd encountered similar rays in a so-called touchpool at a sea-life centre. These rays have not had their stings removed and this is not, I repeat, *not* a touchpool.

It may be, after all, that to the bereaved speaker, as to a storyteller, a peculiar authority befalls. Yet he pauses once more, curious as to how long he can continue without someone, perhaps his aunt, breaking into ridicule, or at any rate passing some kind of comment.

– What do you feed them on? blushes the teenage daughter of another cousin.

– On shrimps, he replies, a little snappily. Fillets of whitefish, trout, river perch, with occasional live food such as earthworms and red mosquito larvae.

– What's a touchpool? asks the small boy still lingering near the lip of the unroofed section.

– A good question, declares the grief-stricken man, in a voice louder and more trembling than he might have wished.

He realises in a flash how careful he must be in his choice of words now, already risen up inside all his hatred

73

for the commercialisation of rays that has, in so many coastal resorts around the world, reduced the experience of seeing to one of touching, as if they were puppies to be stroked or rabbits to have placed in one's lap, um likkel inkydinky strokey. No, he has to rein himself in here – otherwise he will frighten the young boy, not to mention appear quite crackers to this gathered group of friends and loved ones. He must, if only for the sake of a certain decorum, fight against the impulse to spit out the euphemistic and quietly nauseating compound phrase 'touchpool' and denounce in the most vituperative terms all those who have ever been responsible for participating in, *or merely encouraging*, a state of affairs whereby visitors to an aqua-life centre can feel at liberty, or feel even that it is their *right*, to touch these creatures, when all the research stresses that rays have extremely sensitive skin all too readily susceptible to trauma. Still the words rush out of him.

– The last thing in the world you should do to a ray, he says, is stroke it, not to mention exclaim aloud, as I have heard people do in marine-life centres around the world, *Ooh, it doesn't feel like anything I felt before,* or *It feels, ugh, like fondling a giant frog*, or *Just like wet rubber*, and so on. The sooner the world is rid of touchpools the sooner people might start properly respecting these extraordinary creatures. I say the last thing in the world, but (and here his gaze wanders away beyond the church-goers, and beyond the cousin and wife who had been stuck in traffic on the road from London but have now appeared at the door and mutely joined the others) *actually* I have witnessed worse something *even more disgraceful* in the case of a sea-life centre on the eastern seaboard of the United States. An official was seated right beside the touchpool, with a cap pulled down over his eyes, while a group of boys not all that much older than *you*, I shouldn't imagine (his raised right forefinger here directly trained on the cousin's boy near the edge), played at pulling their tails as they went gliding past. The boys thought this was just *such a hoot* and the official, employed it should be said by a company purportedly committed to *the preservation of our great marine world and all the inhabitants of our oceans*, merely maintained a blind eye. They were trying to catch then tug along the rays by their tails, worse than swinging cats, and of course the only reason why these little *horrors*, these *mindless shrimps* who might have taken a different attitude to the whole thing if they had been warned in advance of having testosterone *whipped out of them with piano-wire*, the only reason why they were able to do what they did – besides the grotesque and wilful neglect of the fake-dozing official – was because the stings of these rays had been removed. I allude here to an act of barbarity regarding not just the spines but the bulk of the tails altogether, a barbarity most readily appreciated by visiting one of these marine concentration camps, I choose my words carefully, these commercialised marine torture chambers, and witness for yourselves the amputations and the torture chambers and for the ray, for the rays –

He loses his thread and breaks off what was in danger of becoming a rant. He calls to his cousin and the wife whose name, alas, escapes him, please to come in and have a glass of wine or a cup of tea, as he makes his way across the room to welcome them both.

Then his mischievous aunt, always one for keeping up a comical or embarrassing situation if she can, calls out in a high-pitched theatrical voice:

– And tell us, pray: what are the creatures' names, my dear?

And a few of the mourners laugh and he, suddenly mindful of a family of Jehovah's Witnesses, also known to the aunt (but very far, in fact, from her mind), who were once just an ordinary sad bunch of people but became permanently radiant-faced after getting the glory, replies with all due gravity:

Taylor, Audrey, Hilary and Mallarmé, one male and three females.

Ω

Sometimes a house is bigger than a heart, an apparently crazy thought, scarcely stands to irreason: a house is always bigger. But the thinker of the heart knows that in its pull, voracity, embrace and engulfing power it is at least as colossal as the mouth: it sucks up an ocean, casts out decades, burns down at a quiver forest after forest, searing soaring seeking or holding onto its prey, its inseparable maker, in a valley of kings of its own making. But sometimes a house is bigger. You can huff and you can puff but the walls won't give, making the heart collapse, taking it all in at its own pace, a matter of a minute or a year and the house has prised open the heart and built itself so big inside it sprawls out finally standing alone with the heart pulverised, faked within, beyond repair. She recognises this in you and fears you have no sense of it. You know nothing of this.

Three days after the funeral you drive her to Heathrow. In the receding visibility of the security line winding towards the departure lounge, her green shoes and lower body already gone, she turns back and sees you in tears, but she is always weeping first. It is unclear when you will next see one another, if ever, this miraculous relationship that has been going on already for years; she is fearful for you to the trembling tips of her fingers for what will happen now as you head back down the long road west through the summer dusk anxious already for the creatures abandoned that morning. There is the calm of water-lights, the shade and cool of this other world restfully alert to the eye, buried in time, the placid underworld and prehistoric clarity of sitting beside the great tank and watching. You establish a routine in your solitude as keeper, maintaining the quality of the water with the pH value at seven, and the temperature thermostatically regulated to between 24 and 27°C, ensuring a good supply of oxygen to the tank via the filter outlet, removing faeces and left-over food from the substrate using the vacuum siphon, making regular partial water changes to the tank to avoid the build-up of ammonia, nitrite and nitrate, and of course feeding these creatures, securing the appropriate supplies of shrimp, whitefish, perch, occasionally mussels and squid, as well as earthworms, along with a variety of plant foods such as cucumber and lettuce leaves.

Ω

In the doldrums of grief these blazing dog-days alone unflaggingly you patrol the extensive gardens on a small tractor, cutting the chaotic former lawns back to something resembling a controlled state, weeding the former flowerbeds, assaulting the high hedges toting an electric hedge-trimmer like a machine-gun, sweat pouring off you as you shift load after load of grass and weeds and hedge-cuttings dry as a tinderbox down to the bottom of the garden to stack it up on a fire along with the steady flow of combustible material from inside the house, the innumerable papers bills pieces of correspondence, bits of bereft wood from here or there. In the dazzling heat of these raw grief-days you work with mole-like speed and feverish determination to clear as much as you can of the jungle that was once garden, your father's swards, your mother's joy untended, the flowerbeds infuriated with brambles nettles thistles and other weeds, all orderliness choked up in the two and a half years since she died, and making sorties into the drawing room cupboards and bureau-drawers and edging your way furtively, unsteadily, eyes swimming, before setting foot in the end in your father's study, ruinous reliquary of the all-in archive and bibliography of remains.

You encounter, but it is already too late, your father's things: the sturdy, built-in, ceiling-high shelves of old books never read or read in youth fifty or sixty years ago, gathering dust more or less untouched ever since, the numerous boxes and cases and cabinets stuffed, the diffuse array of small wooden tables, some of them of your father's own construction, and the great oak desk piled high with all the gubbins of the inveterate pipe-smoker and former proof-reader and graphic design artist, the papers, the pens, the rulers and magnifying glasses, the erasers, paper knives, inks, ashtrays, debris of stationery, calendars, jottings, newspaper clippings and other memoranda stretching back twenty-five years or more on the surface of the desk alone, untouched since his wife, some four or five years earlier, acted a madness of Miss Havisham in reverse, blundering into her husband's sanctuary, careering maniacally tipping over tables, pushing over pictures, like the strangely unreal stylised portrait of her father-in-law taken in a photographer's studio in Ealing in the 1930s, scattering papers and implements, tearing down books, since which time he stopped working in his study or stopped retreating there to sit in his melancholy old age, taking temporary respite from the otherwise more or less constant responsibility of looking after his beloved wife, mad as an attic as she was, and never again disturbing the disturbance she had created in that berserk interlude but letting the place be, archive of chaos, overrun by spiders and mice.

You encounter, too too late, not only his collected works already scattered but in the deep drawers of the great oak desk and boxes and cases and cabinets the remains of all else, every letter, document and photograph relating to the family, from birth to death certificate, from toddler holiday snaps to terminal correspondence, and of the lives of your father's father and mother, the last deranging flotsam casting up as from a kaleidoscope of sepia a photograph from Bexhill-on-Sea in full beachwear circa 1920, another of your mother's grandparents, labourers on the farm in Scotland never before or again to be pictured, circa 1890, another of your mother's father's father from the Highland Games even further back, caber-tossingly dark and in the vestiges now yours to keep or consign to the almost daily garden pyre or further trip to the tip. With folders containing heating bills and letters exchanged on the subject of the boiler from a quarter of a century ago, or documentation relating to the extension built and the purchase and sale of the house you had previously all lived in, the bundling up and dispatch is almost automatic, but in the case of more personal relics, however apparently trifling, you can linger and lose all sense of perspective before deciding no, not now, not yet, and returning the folder to its place in the drawer.

It is practically crushing you, this end of the end, the ends altogether, coming together, end upon end of the world of your father and mother and family, house and history to be from now on adrift in your body alone. The end presses your forehead as if it were necessary for material to retreat that can no longer do so, slide away when everything has already gone. You remember a book to which he was strangely attached, called *The Hampdenshire Wonder*, and find it with surprising speed. You blow the dust off and you laugh. You laugh with your father. You feel his laugh in you. You have never read this book and wonder why. He showed it to you perhaps thirty years ago and you vaguely recall immersing yourself in the opening pages but no further. You wonder what he so liked about it. You connect it with the word 'hydrocephalic', which you hear, as you have always done, in the precise humorous intonation of your father.

Ω

Watching is also to be watched, the singular oddity of bearing witness to these creatures sometimes buried and virtually out of sight in the substrate, eyes nonetheless kept free, pricked up like cats' ears, at attention in the quartz sand, again and again picked out after the event the realisation of another creature realising you, and at other times as if electrically surging, a trained-up veritable school of four, unforeseeably together, one by one or in ones and twos, ghost birds flapping up through the water, plapping at the surface and looking, yes, from the wings, in alary formation, indisputably on the watch at you, at where you are if not *at* you, the body rising through the water seen in its pulsing forcing resurrecting swoop, showing its creamy white underside, the gill slits and mouth organised as a smile returning to the world dolphin-like yet phantasmic, this rearing up of a living white sheet of ventral alien face, then the superbly fickle jilting gesture, surfacing or retreating, the flip and show of the dorsal view, the waving through the water of backs dark and gorgeous spotted, another world of eyes, the ocellate gliding, neither peacock, leopard, butterfly nor chameleon, but *motoro*, the rays all four the same variant or morph, name unknown. Following the torrid automatism of war in the garden, traipsing your father's hand-built chicken-wire wheelbarrow full of tinder-dry grass, weeds and hedge-trimmings, like a bier down to the site of the daily fire, and driving out to the municipal tip with yet more filled black bin-liners and objects you can no longer face, sweltering days ending always this pseudo-iterative somnambulism, this delirium between repetition and alteration, in the late afternoon you stop, fetch out a bottle of chilled Aspall cider from the refrigerator, and sit down in your father's favourite armchair, immersed in the rhythms of coming

In the first days after the funeral there are occasional visits or calls from neighbours, further cards of sympathy and calls from family friends. The farmer down the lane offers to help with carting stuff off to the tip and tidying the garden, his wife to collect supplies of food for 'the fish', as she insists on calling them, from the city where, some twenty miles off, you have to get such supplies. Someone else, an old friend of your father, calls and tries to put you in touch with another local man who specialises in house-clearance, to move along the business of sorting out the house. You politely decline all these offers, but when the farmer's wife asks for the second time within that first fortnight when are you going to put the house on the market you struggle to remain courteous. As in the story of the man who cannot go into the street because he is absolutely sure he will kill everyone he meets, you find yourself driven deeper into the solitude that is in any case never yours.

It is while you sit with your Aspall, eyes sunk in the cool shadow-life of the great tank, that you talk to the girl last seen in green shoes. In the calm of water-lights, in this placid lost world of *motoro*, you drift for hours, telling her what you have been doing and thinking, enabling her to follow your life by telephone. When the conversation ends it is always the same. It is time to feed the rays. You relish the almost dissociated pleasure of seeing them seeing food on offer and rising to the surface accordingly, or remaining oblivious, at a distance, like Auden's reindeer, altogether elsewhere, picking up a morsel of whitefish, shrimp or piece of cucumber only after it has come to rest on the substrate. It is strangely compelling to observe them eat while being unable to see what it is they are eating, since their eyes are on the other side of their bodies, the sense suggested of a communication between dorsal and ventral not of the order of vision, and the faintly frightening plates of teeth, the closest resemblance the rays have to their cousins the sharks, as they inexorably imperviously grind up their prey living or dead.

Ω

One day the telephone rings and it is H, asking if you would read something from Shakespeare on French radio. You laugh because she always makes you laugh.

– In French?

– No, darling, in English.

She asks you how you are. You want to tell her that you fear you are going crazy. In fact you merely note your unease at what you call the disappearance of the house.

– You must film it, darling.

You want to say yes, but the word stops in your throat. Instead:

– What is the Shakespeare?

– It is Clarence's dream. Will you do it?

And so a couple of days later, at an hour agreed, the radio station calls and they record you reading, over the telephone:

> Methoughts I was embarked for Burgundy,
> And in my company my brother Gloucester,
> Who from my cabin tempted me to walk
> Upon the hatches. Thence we looked toward England,
> And cited up a thousand fearful times

84

During the wars of York and Lancaster
That had befall'n us. As we paced along
Upon the giddy footing of the hatches,
Methought that Gloucester stumbled, and in stumbling
Struck me, that sought to stay him, overboard
Into the tumbling billows of the main.
Lord, lord, methought what pain it was to drown:
What dreadful noise of waters in my ears,
What ugly sights of death within my eyes!
Methought I saw a thousand fearful wrecks,
Ten thousand men that fishes gnawed upon,
Wedges of gold, great anchors, heaps of pearl,
Inestimable stones, unvalued jewels.
Some lay in dead men's skulls, and in those holes
Where eyes did once inhabit there were crept,
As 'twere in scorn of eyes, reflecting gems,
Which wooed the slimy bottom of the deep,
And mocked the dead bones that lay scattered by.

You hear *methoughts* in your father's playful fashion,
like 'me wife': someone is hearing me thoughts. The
recording is not good. To disguise it they later layer a
crashing of waves over you. You sound as if you are
speaking from the deep, within the tumbling billows.

Ω

The next day you tell me:
    – Shakespeare has been filming the house.
    You had a terrible night and could hardly sleep. You
had a nightmare of unimaginable length and intensity.
You attribute it to your 'marine correspondence' with H.
    – I dream of gravel. I'm going to miss the funeral
because of it. Time's recoiled and we are completely

lost in the logistics of acquiring the gravel, the agitation about having the right kind. It's as if I were dreaming intermittently aware that what's happening is an allegory but I keep forgetting this. The surface of the body is such a strange kettle, I remind you, with no scales, and even the dermal denticles on the dorsal surface affording limited protection at best, the ventral surface another hopeless hazard of sensitivity. We are arguing about it. I tell you I *know* that gravel is already a perversion of the standard natural habitat of mud, sand or silt, and no amount of scientific research will bring a satisfactory resolution to the question of the right *kind* of gravel, granted that *gravel* it needs must be. I know that the very fineness of sand or mud creates an *unsustainable havoc*, filter-blocking and anaerobic in the artificially generated world of a home aquarium. You suggest that there are numerous other, equally important issues to be concerned about, such as the type and quality of water, filters, pumps and so on, but I'm not to be deterred. I accuse you of being no better than the so-called authorities who blandly note the abrasive character of gravel as a minor problem to be avoided, since it can lead to infections of a fungal or bacterial nature. Only as it were in passing do they note that such infections are 'almost inevitably fatal'. The ray is but a trifle, easy picking, so many more in the sea. Like cookies churned out on a factory conveyor-belt: such is the tone. I can see I am upsetting you, comparing you quite unjustly with these scientifically trained specialists and collectors, but I'm on my high horse and haranguing like a crazy man:

– Then there are the online dealers. Replaceable ray, dish of the day, this one or that! Initially set you back a hundred dollars, my friend, but if it arrives damaged or dead, refund guaranteed, we'll dispatch another within twenty-four hours! If, on the other hand, you get it home and it acclimatises and seems happy but after three weeks begins to develop fin curl or abrasions from that gravel you selected for the substrate, or if it turns out the creature never really developed an appetite and has succeeded in starving itself, such apparently suicidal behaviour not unknown, if it dies it dies: just think of it as one of those balloons that go flat, simply pick up the phone or get online and order another one!

– I notice that you have stopped listening and put in your earphones and are playing music, but this only makes me rail the more.

– Nothing sharp that might abrade the creature's ventral surface. That's the main thing. It's hardly a question of driving down to your local gravel pit and filling up the car in a series of stealthy operations: so many black bags filled, like all our recent life in reverse. Obviously it is necessary to realise that there is *no such thing* as aquarium gravel in the plain and simple sense. Nothing is *reliable*. If you spend most of your adult life burying yourself in a mass of tiny rocks you perhaps should expect to get into a few scrapes. But don't imagine the guys at the building supplies company are going to give us much useful information or assistance in a situation like this. We're strictly *on our own*!

– So then I'm sitting on the dining room floor surrounded by bags of gravel, the sort known as quartz sand, with a grain thickness of 0.4 to 1mm. You're nowhere to be seen. Nothing's been done. There's no sign of the frame or any of the other equipment. I'm working my way through, bag after bag. From one bag to the next I inspect every little pebble, taking it like snuff between the thumb, forefinger and middle-finger, feeling, turning and assessing its abrasiveness, accepting or rejecting accordingly. I'm distracted by the thought that among all the hundreds of thousands of tiny granules there may be a few, a child's handful or just one, a solitary single serrated little bastard that will injure and quite possibly lead to death. And I'm going as fast as I can, but all the time I'm thinking to myself: I'm *missing the funeral*.

– Then I wake up. I'm covered in sweat and my heart is thumping like a nightclub. It's pitch dark and I can hardly breathe.

Ω

I call you and begin by asking where you are, even though you are always in the same place. I depend on this routine. As you sit in your father's armchair you can tell me about Mallarmé, Hilary, Taylor and Audrey. It's calming to hear your voice and description of the movements in the pool. But then there's no knowing which way the conversation might go. A couple of days after the gravel-dream (which you tell me comes back repeatedly over the nights that follow, and which you relate to a disquiet you have about 'no substrate at all'), you declare:

– I am going blind.

– What do you mean?

– I mean blind. I catch myself staring, as if I'm simply failing to shut my eyes, and what I see is dissolving. It's as if I couldn't sleep, but I go out like a light. Things appear bright and blurred at the same time.

– That's just what you've been going through, the burden and strain of everything. It will get better. Try to sleep longer tonight. Have a lie-in.

But the thing persists. A couple of days later you refer again to troubled vision and then, after a pause:

– I'm overlooking myself.

Sometimes I wonder if I hear you correctly, your accent foreign and still unfamiliar (doubtless in part that is why I love your voice), an impression accentuated by the telephone and hundreds of miles between us. One cannot endlessly ask, Could you say that again? or Did you say you're overlooking? Signifying what? A surreal game of Whisper Down the Lane tracks our every syllable.

– In France they call it Arab Phone.

– Sounds offensive. What are you talking about?

– No more than calling it Chinese Whispers. I'm sorry, I was thinking out loud. It took a moment to realise you said 'overworking'…

– I didn't. I said I'm overlooking. But you're right, as always, my love: I don't actually know what I meant by it. We might have invented another game: *Overlook*.

– What is this? Shakespeare meets Stephen King?

– Sorry. It's an odd word, I see that. I'm overlooked in my birth.

– I guess you're overlooking the rays.

– Yes, I'm looking after them. But I only meant I have this strange feeling of looking too much, seeing too hard. Like I said, things are blurred and bright at the same time.

– So: go to a doctor or optometrist or whatever.

There follows soon afterwards a torturously lengthy examination process at the local optician's, with the optometrist over-close, fitting the measuring cage to the face, quietly spoken, insinuatingly moralistic:

– And when did you last have an eye-test, sir?

The examination seems interminable.

– I'm now going to shine this light into your right eye, sir. Very bright is it, sir? We're almost done here, if you can just bear with me for a few more minutes. Turn to the right, please: look straight ahead. That's splendid. And to the left...

– Hmm, says the optometrist finally, his breath cloudy in your face: That's not so good.

Yes, finally you are told, your eyes have grown markedly weaker, and new glasses are provided with unexpectedly promptness.

– Are they helping? I ask him in due course, as easy-going as I can.

– Let's wait and see.

Ω

You are an increasing worry, more elusive, desultory. I miss you intensely and wish I could join you but work commitments prevent me for at least three months. In the past we have undergone longer periods of being apart, but now things seem more precarious and difficult.

There's no substrate, you say.

Words appear to you in a dream: 'In the grave you hear no sound / But all the things in the ground.' And then another time: 'The asseveration comes in the night.'

You keep dreaming that you are late for the funeral. You miss it altogether. You miss most of the reception as well, like the cousin who turns up only at the end.

You haven't organised anything properly. You still have to do the gravel. This recurrent nightmare proceeds, you believe, from a sense of outrage at the so-called specialists who have the gall to suggest that there is *no need for a substrate*. It may come as quite a surprise for the creatures on arrival and they will certainly experience discomfort, for they are accustomed to using their pelvic fins for shifting through the substrate and they'll find themselves slipping horribly. But they can get used to it, these specialists imply, as if these creatures that so love to bury themselves, whether out of sudden fear or simply in order to express a deep behavioural instinct, the delight in covering themselves so that only the eyes protrude, and the joy in blowing water into the substrate, to spout up morsels of food, could readily adapt to the imposition of a completely different, nonspecific gravity, the carpet pulled out from under their ghost-white bellies.

I remember when you first mentioned these creatures, around the time of your mother's death. You came to see me, not long after, and said in the car as I was driving us out of the airport that you'd like to visit a sea-life centre of some kind to see if they had any rays. What a strange man, I thought, how I love you. Who else would come out with a remark like that, more or less the first thing you say to someone having not seen them in several months?

And so the next day we located somewhere, in fact one of the oldest aquaria in the country, in a little seaside town a couple of hours' drive away, and sure enough they had a ray pool or, as they called it, a touchpool. It was in that dead period, no longer winter, not yet spring, with a raw wind blowing off the ocean, and we were the only ones there, besides the girl who worked at the aquarium who was feeding them. It was the first of many trips to marine-life centres, but I'll never forget the strangeness of that first time. I don't think I had ever in my life really looked at a ray or given a moment's reflection to the subject. I guess I fed off your fascination, and also caught something from the girl, since she seemed surprisingly well-informed about these creatures and at the same time obviously fond of them. It still feels odd to talk of being fond of rays, I guess, but standing there with you and the girl (despite the freezing cold and grey blank of the afternoon) I came to share something of what you called this 'new imaginary'. I mean, when I looked at these fish, really looked at one, for the first time, up close, in detail: *weird*!

Of course we didn't know at this time about the injurious effects of touchpools. The girl eventually asked would you like to touch one. I said, don't they sting? She said they've had them removed. An image of strange pathos came into my mind: the art of archery, without arrows. It's a constant discombobulation to reflect on what we overlook, for of course then it was plain as day the creatures at the base of their tails featured these pinkish stumps. Your distaste for the trade began right then: I could see it. Driving back to my apartment I saw that you were sobbing. I assumed it had to do with your mother, but all you said was:

– Those pointless stumps!

On later trips to marine-life centres you would often become visibly enraged at seeing the spines had been snipped off, if that's the right phrase. Doubtless an understatement. 'Sawn off' is more apt, more in accord with the brutality of the act, even if it is done with an anaesthetic like Finquel.

The first we witnessed were a cow-nose variety, not the loveliest on the eye, but still they were eerily engrossing. Even then, on that first encounter, when the girl invited you, you wouldn't touch. Already there was a certain reserve in relation to these creatures who were to acquire such centrality in our life. I couldn't simply say they were beautiful, because there is also something uncomfortably negative about them. They're never exactly a happy-go-lucky sight. They always remain wayward. Irreproachably creatures of elsewhere is how I think of them. Even if you are close, as we were that afternoon, to this fellow with a sad stump rendering him completely harmless, and he comes bobbing up through the surface and looks up at you like a blind pet spaniel. You can feel you're infinitely far away from him, but still there's this singular unease he generates. Gazing in a quite detached way, just as you might find yourself other creatures in an aquarium such as sharks, still you get caught up short somehow. You are unable to have a clear impression of what perspective or dimension to look at them from. Are they upside down or back to front, fat or thin, facing you or away? How can this creature be looking at me? Fish don't look at you. Makes no sense.

Neither fish nor fowl, they move like moles in the gravel of the substrate, burrowing and blowing up air, like animated pancakes, or stay at rest on the bottom, half-hidden dark moons. Or they glide through the water like ghosts on a shopping spree in an empty mall. But the otherworldliness is constantly undercut by a kind of normality. They gently bump into one another and shift accordingly, like courteous commuters. They eat with their little plates of teeth, grinding up whatever it is they select as the *plat du jour*. They shit into the watery depths, like muting birds in flight. They indulge in sexual congress, though it was a fair number of visits to sea-life centres before finding ourselves one day, in Portugal, peculiarly a party to that voyeurism.

How to talk about them? They are eerie machines for creating and overturning words. Every time you think you have come up with an appropriate way of describing them, a submarine bird or robotic frittata or psychodelic beret, you are undone. You're mere bystanders. They're Teflon: nothing sticks because in reality they are the cooks, the makers, somnifluent agents of provocation and alterity in a maddening game with invisible rules in operation before you set eyes on them and being perpetually revised. But nothing sparks talking like the constraints of doing so. Our telephone conversations thus find respite of sorts, from the more or less constant anxieties over which we range, regarding nightmares and eye problems, the apparently never-ending business of clearing the house and gardens, and how rawly we experience each other's absence.

Ω

One morning (for it is morning in my time-zone) you sip from your glass of ice-cold Aspall and describe how Mallarmé is nudging up the side of the tank to within a foot of your face. From the patina of ocellation you have learnt to distinguish easily between the rays and, picturing these differences, I have memorised them so that I can follow. Of course the single male is the most immediately identifiable, having claspers.

– It's a completely different world, you say.

I assume you're referring to the pool. But you go on:

– The totter has gone.

I have to cast my mind back.

– The beautiful lionish man: *vanished*! He hasn't been there since we saw him there together, just before the funeral. I meant to tell you. It's a completely different world.

– At the tip?

– Everything is being stripped away. I can't express it. I'm experiencing new, incredible possibilities. It's a kind of magical sharpness, as if shadows have light, and the totter's disappearance belongs to a time that is coming back but for the first time. It has to do with that mimosa thing I told you about. It's a kind of upside-down space of coincidence, a portal. I can't *stay*...

Your voice is strained and I'm having real difficulty following what you are saying.

– What is happening there? Are you missing me?

– I can't *wait* to see you again. But the weirdest thing has just happened. I wonder if I'm not going completely off my head.

A long pause ensues. An expanse of hundreds of miles of deep cold sea dangling the frailty of a telephone is not a reassuring medium for a long-term relationship.

– What do you mean?

– I'll write. I love you.

Then you hang up. I call back but there's no answer.

Ω

There is no internet at the house, but you must have gone, as you sometimes do, to the café in town to write: the Tea Party, as it's quaintly called. For a couple of hours later an email arrives, in which you explain that yesterday afternoon, having just overseen the day's final fire of ripped-   up nettles, clipped brambles, hedge trimmings and scythed grasses, eyes a-blur stinging and watery from acrid smoke, a slight breeze at the fireside an almost pleasurable twisting of a knife swirling smoke one way then another, walking up the steep back lawn towards the house bulking up with almost manorial proportions above you, it occurs to you, a decision precisely contrary to all your desires and hopes. You're going to sell the house. You phone the estate agent and a meeting is arranged. And so this morning the gentleman duly appears and enthuses and proposes an asking price and takes photos, starting with the gardens from this and that boundary or angle, standing on a woodworm-eaten ladder (a big man, perspiring in a suit and tie, trying to get the best photogenic perspective) which snaps clean through under his weight and he tumbles unpleasurably roly-poly down the slope of yellowing grass. And inside he clicks and slicks away at this and that room, deterred only here or there. Naturally, unphotographably, your father's study remains the last stronghold of chaos. The biggest obstacle, of course, is the first thing inside the front door (but Shakespeare, you want to say, is working on it). The agent's lack of surprise suggests he has been tipped off (down in the town things get about). Encountering what was once a dining room now a major aquatic display he blandly enquires what you plan to do with it.

– Not, he queries chuckling, presumably to be part of the fixtures and fittings?

– I'd be taking that with me, you say, struck momentarily by the enormity of doing so.

– What are they in there anyway? asks the man, stooping a little and peering in.

And then one of them, Taylor, flaps into vision, and it occurs to you that you haven't in fact shared the secret of the rays with anyone since the funeral.

– Curious, exclaims the visitor. Like an underwater kite.

There is now a delayed version, you suggest, a shadow-replay of his falling through the ladder five minutes earlier and almost breaking his legs when, his curiosity getting the better of him, the agent goes to put his hand near the surface of the water as Taylor edges up close and you, rallying to the defence of both parties, pull the arm back, exclaiming at the danger of the spine lashing his hand. Stung at any rate mentally, the estate agent remarks that it is not going to be easy transporting a contraption of dangerous creatures that size and you have to agree. Surveying the upstairs rooms he more than once poses the question of the fate of other furnishings and items obviously capturing his business eye.

– Some nice furniture, he remarks. Will you be instructing the auctioneers in town?

A query too far for you at this moment, you merely note you have not yet decided what to do with it, and the agent with newfound gusto and boldness avers that while the condition of the house, so obviously in need of modernisation, is not going to put off a prospective purchaser, given that the price would be tailored to that fact, and while such a person would be attracted as much as anything else by the size of the plot of land coming with the property, nonetheless a bit of tidying up and clearing space in the bedrooms and the drawing room downstairs might be advantageous for the purpose of viewings.

– Your father's study in particular, he sighs with but a thin veneer of professional decency.

He leaves you with the promise of papers to sign, coming with luck in the post next day, and an unnecessarily impactive handshake.

Five minutes later you too drive out, seeking replenishments of your favourite bottled cider.

It happens, or has already begun, on your return. There is a sound coming from the kitchen. You can hear it above the noise made by the water-pump in the pool as you come through the front door. There is, you write, a resting place in every mental archive, a discrete space of effects walled up without a listener's awareness. Most remain unnoticed in the dull daily roar. Then there are the others, those isolated, unmistakable sounds which, once heard again, transport more directly and more frighteningly than any odoriferous power of reminiscence or snapshot visual recall. Of course there is a kind of common stock, shared files of archetypal distinction, the sound of rock falling, a footstep where none is expected, the thrown vocable of a diabolical chuckle, the autumnal rustling of trees, a snatch of distant seas shrugged off in the dozy instant. But there are also sounds peculiarly your own, received and buried, as it were, in your heart of heart. It is what you mean, you remind me, when you tell me I am your pristine.

The sound you hear on coming back through the front door, carrying over the peaceful bubbling of the pumps in the ray pool, is a screech. You recognise it immediately: it is the shriek, initially a scrawny cry but rising, made by your mother locked in the bathroom upstairs one night twenty years ago, shortly after the local GP downstairs administers a final dose of morphine, on the occasion of the first death, the deciding death. And now coming into the house the hallucination, for you tell yourself it could only be such, is that unmistakable but faint cry, started up from you can't think where. It is a savage gutturality, a fugal scree. After a moment of absolute disorientation you think of the upstairs bathroom, where you recall she would not respond to your murmured entreaty but kept up this speechless screech intolerably, forcing you in due course to let her be and return downstairs. Climbing the stairs again now the sound, you note, has outstripped you. The upstairs landing is silent and still. Coming face to face with a bathroom door that is closed, however, re-establishes your disquiet with a sharp, unpleasant flutter. Always in the time of your parents the door of the bathroom, if unoccupied, would be ajar. With trepidation you open it. There is nothing: a once pleasing up-to-date emerald-green bathroom now unequivocally in need of what the estate agent called modernisation, the chrome covers to the taps long since broken off, the cracked cover to the cistern leaning against the wall below the window, the bath and bidet stained bone-grey and cobwebbed. Then you realise it must have been the estate agent, closing the door behind him as he was making his tour of the house.

Ω

Your mother is in the kitchen, sitting at the table.

– Is your father out?

She is sitting with a cup of coffee, with her daily crossword, shopping list and pen on the table, along with her cigarettes, a lighter and ashtray.

– He has died, you say.

– Typical. Is there anything you'd like me to get while I'm down in town?

She has put out her cigarette and picked up her ballpoint to write.

Yes, you think, before or beyond any religious belief, the dead speak. You don't choose them any more than they choose you. Masters and mistresses of restraint, they hardly ever raise their voices. They try, if anything, to keep their commentary in wraps, their interventions airy nothings, their refrains mere janglery. Yet life is mostly a matter of how you listen to them.

– You're smoking again.

– People who don't smoke don't exist.

– But you gave up.

– Once a smoker always a smoker. *When* did he die, did you say?

– Three weeks, no, nearly four weeks ago.

She then fills in a crossword clue, precisely as if she is in a world of her own and has neither spoken nor listened.

– Are you well?

She scrutinises you over her spectacles as you continue to stand, as if paralysed, at the kitchen door.

It is, without a shred of doubt, your mother, restored like the work of an old master, but alive, here in the kitchen, smoking, drinking coffee, doing the crossword, talking to you, apparently capable of driving down to town and getting shopping.

– What of the Alzheimer's?

The moment you utter the word you realise you had never in her hearing done so. You begin now to advance into the kitchen, walking like an invalid, supporting your slow progress by keeping a hand on the counter as you take one step forward, then another. You wonder what has happened to your body.

– *Alzheimer's?* she says, quizzically. That's an invention, dear boy, not my bag at all. Of course it has currency, as you quaintly call it. Don't get me onto currents. I lost my marbles. To each her own. I'm losing my marbles I said to you, I'm sure you remember (at which you nod).

And now you are standing in front of her at the table and trying to take her hands and bring her to her feet and gather her in your arms. And as you do so your strength seems to return. No longer seeing her, you hold, buried in the warren of this embrace, alternately closing your eyes as if to protect them and gazing out through the window at the forsaken ghost of a garden, you regale her with details of everything that has happened up to this moment, since your father died, every nuanced little thing. And you want to tell her what happened to her in turn, what it was to lose face, both of you, your mother no longer recognising you, speaking to the dead mother of a mother living but no longer capable of being addressed.

– The last time I saw you, you whisper at her ear, a weightless wisp of her dead grey hair caressing your cheek, was two and a half years ago and you didn't recognise me. You were in a care home, past caring or

101

home. For months already you were powerless of speech, incontinent, reduced to liquid foods, unable to follow even fragments of conversation. Before that, still here at home, for months and months already you'd lost the plot. You'd sit in your armchair in the drawing room, in wandering glassy-eyed silence for minutes or hours on end, then rise, walk on autopilot through the dining room into the kitchen, stare out through the window, trying to fool an observer into perhaps thinking you were looking at the bird-table where your once-beloved blue-tits, nuthatches and woodpecker might be pecking at the peanuts, perhaps actually looking at the bird-table, perhaps neither looking nor feigning to do so, then walk back to the drawing room and sit again, glassy-eyed again, or else again here, in the kitchen, try to do one of the things you used to be able to do, such as make a cup of coffee or get yourself a cigarette or help yourself to a biscuit from the cupboard. But those days were past. You had to be followed everywhere, in case you fell over or set the house on fire. And you were still his beloved wife. He would come to see you at the care home every day after breakfast, bringing a packet of digestive biscuits and a pocketful of paper kitchen-towels for when you dribbled. He would feed you, just as if you were your birds, and afterwards wipe the dribbling, trembling, futile mouth, over and over, whether or not that morning you were willing or able to munch and crumble. You would scarcely recognise him, giving out, in the early weeks, some sigh or stammer in the semblance of acknowledgement, then not even that. It must have been around then he had his silent heart attack. He claimed you recognised him, right up to the end (and here you talking. You apologise. You tell me you had to stop writing, because the café was closing. And when you got back to the house you were suddenly overwhelmed with an incredible tiredness, as if you hadn't slept for weeks. Omitting even to feed the rays you fell into a sleep as deep as a coma and have only just come to. You say you thought it was in your head, or the estate agent stolen back into the house and playing a trick on you, improbably hiding in your parents' bathroom and producing a top-class imitation of your mother's screech. But how did he know how to imitate her? No: there was no one in the bathroom. The door was closed and you couldn't open it. Not locked, just a window you'd left open had blown the door shut and now the wind was blowing a gale through, keeping the door as if stuck fast and whistling up a sound like a mad fugue, you say, a horrible frenzied feeling subsiding as you heard the screech fade and found the door could, after all, be opened quite easily and the bathroom empty, a site of harmless ruin and cobwebs enlivened by breezes. But then in a state, you say, of high but bleary relief you went downstairs and your mother was sitting at the kitchen table, fresh as reality, puffing on a cigarette, sipping at her coffee, fiddling with the *Times* crossword, quizzing you about your father and asking did you want any shopping as she was planning to drive down to the town. You asked about her Alzheimer's, you say, and suddenly realised you'd never used the word to her face. It was mortifying. You say you were frozen rigid at first but then went closer. You thought you were in Madame Tussaud's. When you first saw her, you admit, it was unpleasant to say the least, like a huge wave of something staggeringly malodorous washing in from the sea. Not this, you thought. You couldn't move. You were stranded at the open kitchen door in a trance, rigid, and would have called me, an ambulance, a neighbour, but so many things seemed to be happening at once. It wasn't just your mother sitting calm as the moon, it was like curtains pulled back very sharply, to expose another veil, one giving way to the next. It was when I said the word 'Alzheimer's', you say.

You were seeing things, you see that. You frame a reconstruction: you're hallucinating, had a funny turn coming back into the house, big day, big decision to sell the place, things perhaps all too quick, calling in the estate agent straight away and his speed taking the pictures, falling through the ladder, getting the sale rolling, as he said, with luck find you a buyer before we even have the brochure printed.

– It's the word 'Alzheimer's'. Its very anachronicity produces the future it traces. Do you think I'm crazy? The moment I say it my mother looks at me, her soul collaborator, innocent little girl's blue eyes she had even when she had completely lost the plot, but looking at me now in complete possession of her senses, entirely derailed by my use of this word, as if I have made a mortally serious mistake and something is being ripped, carefully but very fast, from the top of my brain. I say Yes, I see, Mother, it's not your word, and I'm in tears now and scarcely conscious but we're standing embracing one another, and then I'm lying on the floor. I have wet myself and my mouth is full of the taste of blood. I've bitten my tongue, I realise, coming round, and I see no sign of her or of the paper, the coffee mug, cigarettes or ashtray, not even a whiff of tobacco smoke remaining. I take a shower and feel cold, as if I'm dead myself, like Clarence: as if I were drowned.

Ω

Sometimes in a pool you can see one ray has sort of sidled up along the substrate and come down on another, sort of half-covering her. There's nothing sexual about it *per se*. It's like you can't tell if they're even aware of it. I remember when you suggested they are curiously insensitive in this haptic dimension: they can flop down on a heater, not realise, and get burned. But then they also seem to sense more or in other ways than we do: they are always a turn or more ahead of the game. I guess it's not so incredible. They have massive brains proportionate to the rest of their body-size. They're a great deal more *intelligent*, whatever that word is supposed to signify, than sharks, and sharks are supposed to be pretty smart after all.

It's so difficult not to project onto them what you are thinking and feeling. You see this *motoro*, Mallarmé for instance, lying down as in a bid for amatory adventure, spreading out over Hilary, and Hilary doesn't seem to care an iota, being apparently quite fulfilled in the serenity of the substrate, vaguely nosing perhaps for a morsel of what you dropped into the pool half an hour earlier and Mallarmé, having settled like a spaceship, then does absolutely nothing. You think: why do that? Is it chance that Hilary's at rest just where Mallarmé came down? Is there some surreptitious motive, is it just being friendly or is there nothing in it at all, you can't help but picture with a smile asking yourself, when someone sidles up to you and lays most of their body area on top of you?

And there's something about these creatures that really makes me flip, like a kind of stratifying of the universe which is, after all, in the language of astrophysics, remarkably flat. Watching rays you get to feel this in a truly spooky way. We have shared this, I think, from the beginning. It has to do with the realisation that people have such a ludicrously anthropomorphic ego-projective perception of everything. They can't so much as glance at a fishtank without thinking of being them, inhabiting a watery world of swimming, floating, shimmying through the depths. What must it be like, you think to yourself, to have the constant noise of that water-pump and filter system, the endless inanity of nosing up and down and burrowing in the substrate, and eating whatever is provided when it is provided, and flopping on a fellow-creature if that's how the mood takes you, or burying yourself in gravel: what sort of a life is *that*? And then at the same time you come to experience this quite different thing, the murky registration that, in terms of deep time, in terms of the actual timeframe of life on the planet, half a hiccup ago you were a lungfish yourself. You were decidedly less imposing-looking, but you were a not dissimilar sort of creature yourself. At which point you dimly sense a sort of vast retelling, a turning shadow cast out over the waters in the flickering light of which the projection actually goes *the other way*, and the refractively aleatory antics of Mallarmé with Hilary, no different now from how they would have been a couple of hundred million years ago, show us frankly what or who we are.

Part Three

It is scarcely seven weeks, still less than two months, since the funeral. A week, a month, whizzing in an hour. Every noun is another ephemeroid. Time pop. No more thought bubbles, never again. I miss him and worry more than I can say. He speaks sometimes with his usual lucidity but at other times he sounds somehow off, difficult to follow, obscure. And too often I can't reach him at all. Where have you been? I thought you said you'd be around today? Don't you remember I said I'd call at this time?

I tell him he has to see a doctor.

– About the episode?

He calls it the one-off episode, like it was a special edition of a TV show. He assures me he will go. And then for three days I hear nothing. Three oceans. He doesn't answer the phone, he doesn't respond to emails. I send half a dozen text messages imploring him to let me know he is OK. On the fourth day he picks up the phone and sounds normal. He asks how I am, apologises for not being in touch earlier, he's been out a lot, tootling about in the motor, he says, picking up supplies for the rays.

– I'm onto a new project, he says.

– What about the doctor?

Silence. Then in a dipped voice:

– You'll be just like the rest of them. You'll think it absurd. I have a new theory of ghosts. It's been staring me in the face.

His voice sounds strained. I try to reassure him:

– Of course not. I'm listening, my love.

Then he pitches off again:

– I was down at the Tea Party... Oh!

– Whatever's the matter?

– Oh, my god! It's happening again!

– What are you saying?

– It's the rays. I noticed it last time we talked and now it's happening again. I was just feeding them some bits and pieces of left-over salad from the fridge. They were tranquilly engaged with that, chomping away, then when the phone rang...

– Yes, when the phone rang?

– It's as if your voice, that pristine chapel, held in place, hello?

Another silence.

– Are you there?

– It's like a choreography written in water. When you speak they raise themselves up, as if braced by something deep inside your voice. They were busy at the lettuce but the moment I say 'Tea Party' they all break off, and when you go 'Whatever's the matter?' perk up their noses and pulse upwardly through the silvery light of the pool, in a shimmy of adoration. They miss you.

I laugh, a bit apprehensive, unsure how much of this is his English sense of humour.

– I miss *them*. You were at the Tea Party...

– ...having a coffee and veering about on the net, I came across all these images of rays, you have to see them. They're stunning. But then there's something that's terrible. It sickens me. It's from somewhere, some hunting grounds I want to say, off the coast of *your* country. I *don't* want you to see this. It's like the forbidden photograph in Barthes, the most important one, he doesn't reproduce. It's almost a hundred years ago and there's this moustache-twirly sea captain standing in front of a dead ray that's been yanked up on a crane, perhaps an old fire-engine winch. It's a manta. A 'giant devil fish', as the silly caption exclaims. It measures seven metres across and weighs eight tons. For me, it's a photograph of photography. It's a puncturation of the punctum. It's a riddle, a true riddling: a punctum everywhere you look. It's the astonishing, majestic corpse of a manta, bigger than any living creature. It fills the frame and it's full of bullets: it seems the creature caught its hunters rather than vice versa. It comes with strings attached.

– Strings attached?

– Strings, lines, ropes, yes: it got caught up in fishing lines and the noble captain and his trigger-merry men had to shoot it twenty or thirty times to be confident it was dead, but it's a picture that shows you the ropes, the way everything is rigged. The colossal creature is strung up: the iconography of a lynching is unmistakable. And the captain is standing proprietorially alongside, pointing with his right forefinger, in case you might otherwise not notice the – I was going to say, elephant in the room.

113

Like a tenting to the quick, now dead, his digit is itself a wound. *Ecce Manta birostris*. Another wound, but not the last. And can you guess what he's holding in his *other* hand?

– His gun? A cigar?

– At first glance it looks like a paper plane. But it's a baby manta, rigid, barely ten inches across, stillborn, proudly extracted from the mother at the creation of the massacre. And then the eye...

– I, ego?

– No, this isn't about the ego. The eye of the photograph. It's a way aloft, unnoticed at first amid the ropes and crane, against the tall deadwall blankness of brickwork that forms the backdrop to the whole picture. Only one is visible, but it's the mother's eye, and it's looking at you, just as though it were alive.

– Sounds terrible. It reminds me of something I was reading recently about hypnosis. Just as you can never be sure someone under hypnosis isn't merely pretending to be, so a dead eye in a photo might be a *trompe l'œil* too. I'm sorry. But I was asking you about the doctor...

– No, my dearest, I'm telling you about the new project.

– But I'm asking *you* about the doctor...

– You wouldn't believe what I've managed to do here. I've been working at it day and night. It's a new pool.

– What do you mean, a new pool?

– Well, not 'pool' exactly. More like 'donut'. Ah! They're doing it again! Incredible! When you said you were asking me about the doctor, when you put the stress on 'you', they started choreographing you again. Hilary gave this sort of twitch of grace and went sliding, jetting

114

– You want to know about the doctor? Exactly. Everything's fine. My brain's entirely normal: that was their actual phrase. I signed up in town as a temporary resident and saw the doctor and he set up a hospital appointment for me the very next day. It was like being in a very slow washing-machine. And then the letter came through from the consultant just yesterday. I'm all clear. I'm *entirely normal*! But here's the thing. And it has to do with the photograph I was telling you about. It's about ghosts and nakedness and superimposition. When I signed on at the local surgery I'd expected to see the GP who saw my father, but actually it was the old one, the other one, the doctor who used to be our family doctor, twenty years ago. Dr Scrivens is his name. He's always given me the creeps. My mother couldn't tolerate the thought of him and when she began to decline, through the disintegration of days and years following the point at which as she told me she was losing her marbles, she connected keeping her health with not seeing this doctor, and then the question came up of her seeing him. It would have been a sort of declaration that she was certifiably off her rocker. The whole prospect terrorised her. It delayed for weeks the very idea of getting her seen by anyone at all. In the end my father managed to get her transferred to another doctor. But then on some later occasion, to do with a graze on her leg that would not heal, my father took her along, sitting with her in the waiting room before guiding her through the door when called, virtually into the arms of Scrivens. Floating face-up in Alzheimer soup was she by then merely oblivious? Or did seeing this object of terror somehow return *her* to life, in the way that sometimes a tiny incident or chance encounter can trigger a massive recuperation, if only for a moment? All of this only comes back to me now when I find myself in the same trap. I am at the surgery and before I realise what's happening there I am, just six feet away from him, and of course he has been expecting me, he's had time to prepare, but our encounter is the strangest phantasmagory, his eyes shifting eerily into focus like binoculars on a death-camp. Naturally he smiles, and I too. It is Scrivens, unmistakably, twenty years later yet miraculously aged, as if from a fairytale. And perhaps he, almost completely gray-haired, fainter-eyed, experiences from head to toe the passage of a similarly wayward vibration: I will look twenty years older to him too. And any second, I know, because now it comes back to me, he'll do that thing with his eyes, that ocular passover, coming out with the standard portrait, the medical gaze that all doctors are trained to impose. But for that crystalline split-second slice of replay, in which we set eyes upon the other, I'm seeing Scrivens in my mind's eye seeing me, double strangers both, outstaring ghosts. That's when I have this eureka thing, and I realise my theory.

Ω

What convinces me that he is having a breakdown? It is not when he goes on to outline the beautiful bareness, as he calls it, of his theory. Nor, perhaps more surprisingly, is it a few minutes later, when he drifts off into what, to anyone else, might seem demented singsong.

It is a question of veils, capes, sheets, shrouds, cloaks, blankets, quilts, mantles.

It's too crazy for a cult. He realises that. And it might indeed remain for centuries illegible, incomprehensible or even imperceptible to the general public.

But a ray doesn't constitute an analogy or 'lively metaphor' for a ghost. Rather, it is the other way round: it is necessary to think spectrality *starting from the ray*. There is no ghost without a trace of the ray. Everything that might be identifiable with the singularity of a living cape or gliding sheet comes back to this. Put crassly, the pallid underside of a ray is not *like* the bed-sheet whiteness of a spectre. The ray is at the origin. It's the originary spook. Plato was already onto that, in the ray haunting Socrates and Meno. What people call the Gothic is a kind of anamorphic manifestation of the effects of the ray. The whole sprawling industry of ghosts and vampires is, in truth, largely a ray-phenomenon. Any moderately reflective reader might notice the importance of cloaks, mantles, shrouds, shawls and so on in the Gothic novel. It is necessary, however, to realise how integrally, how inextricably, this motif is folded into the figure or property of the ray, the living blanket or quilt. The bat is a red herring, in fishy phrase, dried and smoked, tried and tested, a making small and manageable of what is neither. What haunts is of greater scope, more minatory and dangerous, all-enfolding, from another element.

Broadly speaking, the *manta* and the *vampire* (or 'vampyre', in its earliest orthography) emerge at the same period, in the first half of the eighteenth century. That the latter (a fantasy) seems to owe something to the former (the real) might veritably be classed a no-brainer. We don't know when exactly the word 'manta' (meaning 'blanket' or 'cloak') was first used to designate the rays now linked with that name, but it appears to have been originally used interchangeably with 'quilt'. In Socratic spirit it is tempting to construe 'quilt' here in its other sense, namely as a reference to that point in the throat at which swallowing becomes involuntary, but Antonio de Ulloa in his *Voyage to South America* (1758) writes of the ways in which the negro slaves off the coast of Panama are fastened with ropes and forced to fish for pearls, 'and the mantas, or quilts, either press them to death by wrapping their fins about them, or crush them against the rocks by their prodigious weight'. This is as shocking an evocation of the reality of slavery as it is a fictitious and absurd description of mantas. Despite their often great size, manta rays are of course completely harmless. De Ulloa goes on: 'The name manta has not been improperly given to this fish, either with regard to its figure or property; for being broad and long like a quilt, it wraps its fins round a man or any other animal that happens to come within its reach, and immediately squeezes it to death. This fish resembles a thornback in shape, but is prodigiously larger.' It seems unlikely that, for all his luminous childlike gifts as an actuary of the imaginary, Lewis Carroll had the ray in mind when he frabjously unveiled his portmanteau but, once the double meaning of 'manta' is registered, it seems equally difficult not to envisage such a creature in the bag, so to speak, or lurking at any rate under his cloak. It is a question of a new imaginary, not a regression into the vagary of animistic belief, a restituted primitivism, but a thinking of the ray as a force, a trace, whether buried or dancing, in a quite different understanding of the spectre and the wake. Like a dream of excarnation without any possible fossilisation, dream as impossible fossil, there is a naked cape and it is alive. Rays to the ground: starting off in the substrate. It is a matter of a new teratology, an enantiodromic animism that is radically non-theological, nanothinking through the ray.

But next thing he is framing snatches of Clarence, speaking of ten thousand men that fishes gnawed upon, wedges of gold, great anchors, heaps of pearl, his internal marination, lengthening after life, in search of the empty, vast, and wand'ring air.

Gently I ask him what he's talking about, but he's hopped into blurred song, and I am inclined to think this is his way of acting off the slightly 'possessed' sense that he claims his theory has given him:

It's raining, it's pouring, the old man is snoring, I see the doctor, I see the doctor and couldn't get up in the morning, it's roaring, marauding, we went to bed and deformed the head, of hearing and hoarding, who's moaning, who's speaking, it's raining, it's pouring, it's howling, it's calling, the moon rings, the moon sings, it's paining, it's spawning, wedged your head and went to bed, it's feigning, it's shoring, you hear the words are calling, cawing, they're gnawing, and can't get up in the can't get up in the staining, it's boring, she's reigning, he's fawning, I hear your voice, I know you're dead, and can't get up in the morning the morning the morning.

Such is the range of his more lyrical and impassioned traits. There's nothing out of the ordinary here, I think. No, the horrifying conviction comes when he tells me about some writing project he's begun elaborating and proceeds to read it aloud to me over the phone. It is a work of lexicography devoted to the buried life of anagrams and homophones, each word with its own idiosyncratic definition, a dictionaray, yes, as he is pleased to declare: the world's first English dictionaray. It would be a verbal laboratory, a dictionary testamentary to the way the ray leaves its mark in everyday language, a vocabulary that might constitute a new species of bestiary, and generate an altogether other estuary English. He remarks that it is practically impossible to complete, particularly on account of the peculiarity of the adverb form in English, interminably stirring up as it does new terrain. And then he begins. With each new letter of the alphabet he pauses momentarily, then proceeds to the next series of words, giving each entry equal measure, enunciating throughout with customary care and scrupulosity (no doubt, it occurs to me, also his father's). He reads it, in short, precisely in the manner of a poem. It takes me a while to get a grasp of what is going on:

A

Airy
Awry
Anniversary
Anteriority
Arraign
Arrange
Actuary
Afraid
Allegory
Amatory
Arty
Abrasion

Aurally
Absurdity
Already
Astronomy
Astrophysics
Arbitrary
Acrylic
Antiquary
Archetype
Archetypal
Apparatus
Alteration
Alterity
Abruptly
Army
Attractively
Admirably
Articulately
Apparently
Angry
Aleatory
Archaeology
Archery
Astray
Adversary
Ashtray
Aviary
Adoration
Anticipatory
Apothecary
Approvingly
Alary
Adultery

Adulterate
Asseveration
Accordingly
Accurately
Accelerate
Anywhere

B

Brae
Beray
Brain
Bleary
Binary
Betray
Berate
Brassy
Brazen
Braised
Barbarity
Break
Breakdown
Brake
Boundary
Braid
Bray
Brave
Balustrade
Battery
Brutality
Barely
Brace
Barley

Broadly
Beret
Bibliography
Biography
Bastardy
Brandy
Barmy
Bakery
Braille
Bestiary
Bizarrely
Brainy
Birthday
Bystander

C

Crafty
Centenary
Charade
Crystal
Chrysalis
Coronary
Carry
Combinatory
Category
Circularity
Culinary
Chivalry
Courageous
Concentration
Craven
Crayon
Cranny

Crazy
Contrary
Carvery
Centrality
Crane
Cranky
Crape
Crate
Crater
Consecrate
Creatively
Celebrate
Corroborate
Collaborate
Courtyard
Cradle
Crassly
Customary
Carpentry
Cartography
Carefully
Contradictory
Churchyard
Chrysanthemum
Commentary
Cinematography
Crayfish
Chlamydospore
Canary
Charmingly
Comfortably
Creamy
Cannery

Calibrate
Clairvoyant
Clearly
Carbohydrate
Cartilaginously
Certifiably
Constrain
Constraint
Certainty
Conspiracy

D

Derange
Diary
Dairy
Dictionary
Deprave
Dreary
Draughty
Deliberate
Deliberation
Drained
Disgraceful
Driveway
Desecrate
Dray
Drape
Derail
Disparity
Democracy
Dreamy
Dromedary
Debauchery

Dilatory
Decorate
Defloration
Dearly
Disarray
Dysphoria

E

Enrage
Exploration
Exploratory
Exhortatory
Extraordinary
Essayer
Earnestly
Entreaty
Errancy
Extravagancy
Erratically
Exaggerate
Eternally
Embrace
Experimentally
Estrange
Estuary
Early
Erase
Eraser
Entrails
Electrically
Entrain
Elementary
Exasperate

Extraneous
Eccentrically
Everyday

F

Frail
Frailty
Fragrant
Fragrancy
Freight
Fraternity
Freaky
Feathery
Fakery
Foray
Frugally
Fairytale
Fray
Frenetically
Faraway
Fainter-eyed
Fearsomely
Friday
Forsythia
Figuration
Foolhardy
Factory
Ferryboat
Frabjously
Frame
Framework
Filtration

G

Granary
Grange
Gyrate
Generate
Generically
Gray
Gravy
Grassy
Great
Grate
Granny
Grail
Grave
Graveyard
Graveside
Grain
Grammatology
Grammatically
Gravity
Gutturality
Grade
Grace

H

Hairy
Hoary
Hydra
Hydrate
Hilarity
Hysteria
Hysterical

Husbandry
Hairspray
Hearsay
Hardy
Holy-water
Hardly
Hierarchy
Hearty
Harmony
Heraldry
Hydrocephalic

I

Infirmary
Innovatory
Iconography
Irate
Irritably
Irascibly
Iracundity
Idiosyncratic
Infiltrate
Incorporate
Interchangeably
Irenically
Irrecoverably
Irreconcilably
Irreproachably
Ironically
Irradiate
Imagery
Incommensurably
Improbably

Irreciprocally
Irrecognisably
Irrealisably
Irrefutably
Irremediably
Irreparably
Invariably
Irrevocably
Irrecoverably
Irresolvably
Irrationally
Intolerably
Insuperably
Inextricably
Integrally
Involuntary
Illustrate
Inspirationally
Imaginary

J

Jay-walker
Jaybird
Jubilatory
Judiciary
Juratory
Jeopardy
Jellygraph
Jar-fly
Jaspery
Janglery
Jaculatory
Jaw-breaker

K

Kleptocracy
Klydonograph
Karmadharaya
Kirn-baby
Kirkyard
Knavery
Karstology
Kir royale
Kindheartedly
Knick-knackery
Kraken

L

Lairy
Lexicography
Laboratory
Law-breaker
Lavatory
Laundry
Layer
Lay-priest
Lawyer
Larynx
Lycra
Leathery
Largely
Lapidary
Literary
Library
Labyrinth

M

Marry
Metaphoricity
Maternity
Moderately
Meanderingly
Military
Maturity
Mortuary
Mortality
Morality
Migraine
Miraculously
Minatory
Momentary
Membrane
Mammary
Materiality
Myriad
Monarchy
Metaphorically
Marshy
Marvellously
Matrimony
Matronym
Matriarchy
Masturbatory
Moustache-twirly
Migrate
Mastery
Martyr
Martyrdom

N

Narrate
Narrator
Nearly
Narcolepsy
Nocturnally
Nocturnality
Narrowly
Naturally
Nary
Narky
Normality
Necessary
No-brainer
Nearby

O

Obituary
Osprey
Outrageous
Orally
Olfactory
Observatory
Ossuary
Orthography
Ordinary
Ordinarily
Oligarchy
Oragious
Oration
Originary
Originally

Overarchingly
Obliterate

P

Penetrate
Probability
Pray
Praise
Prate
Portray
Portrait
Probably
Purgatory
Psaltery
Phrase
Palaeography
Paternity
Parry
Prostrate
Prey
Pastry
Pregnancy
Preparation
Parade
Perpetually
Particularly
Proprietorially
Presumably
Parley
Patronym
Perpetrate
Photography

Parody
Parity
Pornography
Puncturation
Paralyse
Paralysis
Pterodactyl
Privacy
Pearly
Pleasantry
Primary
Pyramid
Phantasmagory
Pignorate
Prodromally
Paratactically
Perseveration

Q

Quarry
Quandary

R

Ranarian
Rabies
Restrain
Race
Racy
Rabbity
Radiate
Radiator
Radiant

Raise
Raven
Rayon
Radically
Ratio `
Rationally
Rationality
Relay
Replay
Rarity
Rarely
Rain
Rainy
Raincoat
Raspy
Raspberry
Refrain
Reign
Res
Raid
Raider
Ratty
Royal
Rake
Rape
Raze
Rave
Raving
Rally
Ready
Respiration
Range
Rate

Rail
Railing
Ravenously
Rabidly
Rage
Really
Retrait
Remonstration
Registration
Reify
Radar
Raisin
Rapier
Raison d'être
Rein
Refractively
Relatively
Rivalry
Revealingly
Regrettably
Randy
Raunchy
Rascally
Realty
Rotary
Reliquary
Regenerate
Refrigerator
Rampantly
Ramifying
Rainbow
Rhapsody
Reality

S

Secretary
Strange
Stranger
Strangeways
Sharky
Starry
Stray
Spray
Soothsayer
Synastry
Starkly
Strawberry
Spectrality
Straight
Separate
Separately
Spectacularly
Spirogyra
Scrape
Sunray
Saturday
Scarcity
Singularly
Singularity
Strategy
Strategically
Saturate
Serrate
Scary
Swarthy
Syrah

Stationary
Stationery
Staggeringly
Swaggeringly
Scarry
Scarificatory
Similarly
Satisfactory
Sharply
Sedentary
Substrate
Scrawny
Savagery
Stratify
Sanctuary
Skyward

T

Terrain
Trace
Temporary
Tardy
Tarry
Tertiary
Testamentary
Testificatory
Terrestrially
Temporality
Tolerate
Transparency
Trait
Traitor
Train

Training
Trainers
Tirade
Teary
Trade
Tawdry
Tranquillity
Tranquilly
Thermostatically
Taciturnity
Tray
Trail
Tragically
Trimethylamine
Thursday
Tyranny
Tyrant
Translatably
Tyrannosaurus
Timeframe
Topography
Typography
Treaty
Traipse
Teratology

U

Unitary
Upbraid
Unpleasurably
Uranus
Unforeseeably
Unphotographably

Untranslatably
Urbanity

V

Vary
Venerate
Voluntary
Verticality
Variety
Veterinary
Vampyre
Vagary
Veracious
Vestiary
Veracity
Vibration

W

Weary
Wary
Watery
Wayward
Wraith

X

X-ray

Y

Yesterday
Yarn
Yard

Yare
Year
Yearn

Z

Zoography

$$\Omega$$

I listened without the slightest expostulation or inter-vention. What struck me most of all was the tempo and tone in which he read. It remained so steady throughout. And the rendition of each and every one of these words was faultless. It was as if he had been rehearsing it for a very long time. I kept expecting him to change tone, to make a joke, to pause to comment on a particular word, to stumble, to laugh, to groan, to give up. But he carried on in this deadpan manner, as if each word were a world of its own, with its own *raison d'être*. The cumulative effect was like a tide coming in too quickly. He sounded, as he read the thing out, so 'entirely normal', to recall his phrase. Yet something irrevocably strange took place in his relaying of this lexicon, and I know my involuntary intake of breath, in the ensuing blankness, was audible enough for him to pick up:

– What's the matter?

– You were reading so strangely!

– I wasn't reading.

– What do you mean?

– I don't have anything written down yet: I was making it up as I went along.

143

Ω

Something in me gave way. Our separation was no longer to be tolerated. The eerie framing of rationality, this new English dictionary on hysterical principles, this division of voices and hearts of hundreds of miles of cold deep sea made me realise that he couldn't be left alone any longer. I told him I was coming, I'd take unpaid leave or something. I got the next flight I reasonably could, just two days later. I spoke to him only on one further occasion, when I called to let him know my arrival time at Heathrow, and he said he would meet me. It wasn't the best line. I remember saying it's not the best line and he thought I said best man. And at another moment he talked of a 'real surprise', so I thought, but actually it was, as he had to clarify, 'getting ray supplies'. Then he said, if I heard correctly, that he was 'after life' or 'after my life' or 'more life': the reception was very poor. The line went dead, or possibly he hung up. I called back but got no answer.

Bizarrely, he wasn't there. I spent two increasingly anxious hours at Heathrow waiting for his lovely face to show in that great mélange of human bodies crossing and crisscrossing the arrivals hall, calling him repeatedly on my phone, and even having his name paged over the PA system. I was sick with worry by this point. I took trains across country as far as I could. It was a beautiful early autumn day. At last I got out and dragged myself and suitcase up the main street to the Tea Party, having taken it into my head that he might just be there. I don't know what I was thinking – that he was writing me? that he was hiding? I was shattered from the journey and felt an unwelcome but immense desire to lie down and sleep. I took a taxi up to the house. I knew where the spare key was, but didn't need it. Still I rang the bell and stood there a while, as the cab reversed away back up the driveway. I walked inside to what seemed at first like complete normality and put down my luggage.

Charmingly lit and clear, as if waiting to be remembered in every finicky detail, was the great ray pool. I looked into the silvery water and soon enough made out Hilary, Taylor and Mallarmé. Melted clocks, but with a military air, they propelled to the surface, breaking it one two three in a splishing so suggestive of comic applause I couldn't not smile. And Audrey? As if on cue, prodromally precise, a modest but giveaway ruffle in the substrate just nearby where I was crouched: pancaking in reverse, gliding, jetting up, she joined the others. I realised I was already seeing them as he had supposed, a truly radical gymnastics, the pyrotechnic forecasting, irrepressibly pulsing upwardly, from imperceptible in the substrate to shooting up, happy-slapping ghosts, dreamily clowning the surface, unclear who would have been watching who or when, questions ramifying only after the winging off and away, in conversational shadowings. Jetlag was getting the better of me. For a brief interval, which might have been ten seconds or ten minutes, I stared, eyes adrift in the immeasurably engaging turns, breaks and suspensions enacted by the rays as they nuzzled, untroubled in the substrate, plooping up an occasional pebble on a spout of water, then raised themselves up, thrusting, sweeping, surging in exhortatory mime, before surfacing so soft and inhuman, full of gratulatory curiosity.

I got to my feet feeling as if I'd been drugged. I called out his name, three or four times, but my voice seemed eerie and out of place. Although a part of me was worrying that he'd fitted again and fallen someplace in the house, and another part was fearing even worse, I also felt strangely sure that he wasn't there. I was making my way towards the stairs when I noticed for the first time that there was light coming from the drawing room. Momentarily remembering, I opened the door onto that extraordinary affair to which he had (quite earnestly, it was now clear) made reference. The room had been transformed into the interior of a maelstrom, emptied and reorganised in such a way that you walked into a kind of calm, gigantic horse-shoe of water. I could see straight away that it was based on the donut from Barcelona, except that here in the centre was a circular couch, surrounded from floor to ceiling by water. On the couch lay a single sheet of paper. It was in his beautiful hand. Impersonally addressed, I could feel his eyes glittering with pleasure over it. Under the heading 'Eagle rays (*Rhinoptera bonasus*)', it simply offered a list of names together with a short description of their diet and where such foodstuffs could be obtained, along with brief guidelines on the upkeep of the tank. There were twelve names inscribed, as follows:

Larry
Gary
Harry
Andrea
Lorraine
Hardy
Cary

polished wooden floorboards, a new sofa and armchair, family paintings on the walls, and a filing cabinet. By the window, looking out, I realised also how much had been done to the garden. At the other end of the corridor I pushed on the door: his own bedroom was vacant, not even the bed remained. Once more I called out his name, and heard nothing but the absurdity of my own voice.

As I walked back along the midday twilight of the corridor, I felt, tingling in my eyes, virtually breaking me down at every step, exactly what lay beyond. As I opened the door of his parents' room the light seemed at once to stream in and hold. Tears were running down my face. It was a translucent cave. It was crazier than anything downstairs, perhaps in part because of its elevated location. It is part of the law of probability, Aristotle said, that many improbable things happen. What used to be the en-suite bathroom was now incorporated with the bedroom into a remarkable belvedere. The floor must have been reinforced, I told myself. And as I did so, I felt again an estranging taciturnity in the sound of my voice, even within the space of my own head. I gazed up into the depths. The sky had disappeared. It was a manta, the biggest ray, the strangest thing I had ever seen in a house. It seemed, indeed, bigger than the house, arching like a rainbow, majestically large, its great wings black and thin, conforming exactly with that cloak concealing nothing that its name implies. It was hanging, yes, in the watery light, but not motionless. The great pectorals like a double parabola, undulating, arching, in curvy pulsions, the sweeping down of a horseless highwayman, black as night, white as forest snow, it moved at once too easily, slowly and quickly to take in. It was in motion, but it barely moved. Hypnotic: yes, suspended. From the eversion of its underside it seemed to gambol like a lamb. And then it was a bizarre lover fetching invisible pastry straight from the bakery, wearing floppy black oven-gloves. Interminably in need, wherever was I to source the plankton and the nanoplankton? As if dissolving once again, gently shrugging off into a new form, chalk verticality, raft into the shadows of the underworld, veracity in black and white, it seemed momentarily to swing towards me with inhuman inquisitiveness, nudging against my vision, proffering its paddle-like cephalic lobes, head-wide mouth and staggering great white belly with five long slashes of gills. I looked around for some kind of note, a letter, the briefest message, but there was no sign of anything anywhere.

THERE is something at once comforting and strange about the idea of an afterword to a novel. This would be the place where, like dust settling after the massacre, the author considers what happened. Holding out the promise of some illuminating information or ideas about the foregoing pages, the afterword is also, by convention, happily brief: it is a 'word', after all, not 'words'. In these respects the afterword, the very appearance of the word 'Afterword' on a new page near the end of the book, is a reassuring sign: relax, everyone, the novel is over, and what follows is just an add-on. You can take it or leave it. This last bit, if you like that sort of thing, offers an easy-going transition or exit out of the book.

A number of questions nonetheless linger and complicate this enterprise. Does the afterword truly come after the novel or before, especially given its apparent concern with why or how the work came to be written? Is the author of the afterword simply *the same* as the author of the novel? What happens if he begins by solemnly declaring that he is *not*? (I hereby promise: I am not.) What happens if he starts talking or writing like one of the characters or narrators in the book and gradually convinces us that this is in fact who he is? Or if he steadily persuades us that he (or she) is a quite new and different being, but no more or less real than anyone we encountered in the preceding pages? Are we so sure, after all, that what we were reading *was* a novel? And is it so certain that the afterword is not a peculiar continuation of it?

The novel is a space of play. In the past, questions of this sort have generally been part of the entertainment. Writing in the eighteenth century, Richardson, Smollett and Defoe (or their narrators) provoke questions about the novel's truth, identity and seriousness from the start. In those days it was the preface (or some prefatorial equivalent), rather than an afterword, that raised such issues. We tend to take the playfulness of such prefaces for granted today, and conversely look to an afterword in expectation of a certain earnestness and authenticity. In recent decades we had the 'death of the author' to contend with, but we recovered from this or, at least, we like to suppose the author recovered. False alarm, folks – and, if you want evidence of the author's vitality and genuineness, one of the first places to look is the afterword to a novel! The fact that there is today an apparent preference for the afterword might suggest a curious conservatism in reading, or a firmer policing of the way in which novels are organised and their inherent delinquency controlled. The potential of a preface to mislead the reader is dispatched; the afterword seems a more restrained, less worrying genre.

But perhaps we have not yet really begun to think about the strangeness of the afterword as a genre – about its ability, for example, to unsettle the reader's sense of time and causality, to alter the conception of the author, and to threaten or put further into disarray distinctions between fiction and non-fiction. The afterword might thus begin by pointing out that it is the preface that is really the backward genre, since it is invariably written after the work to which it refers: the preface is conventionally just an afterword in disguise. Whereas an afterword (this one I am beginning to imagine here) is a quite crazy thing in which anything could happen. It might go *anywhere*. It might easily turn out to be *longer than the work preceding it*. It might even seek to inaugurate a new kind of writing and give it a name: *reality literature*.

A novel has to do what it has always done: tell a story, give pleasure, compel and surprise us. But the situation of 'the novel today' is singular and unprecedented. It faces challenges and pressures unimaginable in earlier times. It is difficult not to think of writing a novel as an offensive, at best risible instance of 'fiddling while Rome burns' – in other words, while a world war rages all around, with the control and ownership of Jerusalem at its heart, more of the world's population than ever before live in poverty and hunger, women more or less everywhere continue to be positioned as inferior members of the human race, the environment of the planet is being systematically and rapidly destroyed, and non-human animal species are being wiped out daily. How is the novel to respond to this, while trying to do what it has always done? What are a novelist's responsibilities in this context?

And at the same time 'the novel' itself has become so much a mere product, part of the ubiquitous programme. This programme operates on multiple levels, from the creative writing workshop ('how to get your novel published') to the inexorable machine of the publishing industry and the so-called 'global marketplace' (itself, obviously, a fiction), whereby every kind of book of fiction for every age and interest group can be categorised and distributed, bought and consumed, filtered and effectively neutralised. At the core of this programme is the simple but crucial determining principle: a work of literature is merely literature; a novel is *just a novel*. A novel can be as 'original', 'brilliant', and whatever other admiring adjectives you fancy, it can win a 'fiction prize', be talked about on TV, become a movie, so long as it doesn't interfere with the running of the programme, so long as it can be satisfactorily filtered and neutralised, so long as it passes through without making any real trouble *in and with language*.

In the case of a work written in English the prospect is especially acute, for this language ('international English' or 'Anglo-American') is the imposing medium of freedom, as well as of inequality, hegemony and exploitation across the world. This language makes, on millions of people, insidious demands. It is oppressive and domineering, as well as a means of help towards a 'better life' – a fuller education, more rewarding job, widening of horizons, etc. Anglo-American is the language in which democracy, international law and human rights continue to be extended, while also remaining the *lingua franca* of imperialist exploitation and global capital. No language today is more poisoned and treacherous.

But, for the English novel, this is also its chance. The novel has to make trouble *in and with language*. It must meddle. The novelist has to aspire to a writing that figures and insists on strangeness, on what cannot be appropriated or turned over to the language police. The novel has to resist and, as far as it can, interfere with the smoothly neutralising, nulling flow of the programme. It must strive for English to appear in its most pristine form, as what it always was: a foreign language. It would thus urge a new experience of that language, inviting readers to feel for themselves the strangeness of this 'English' which, after all, belongs to no one. Meddling and strangeness, however, should not be confused with calculation and coldness. The novel must also be a work of love. Which means speed. It means moving, in Shakespeare's words, 'with wings as swift / As meditation or the thoughts of love'.

The novel can seem such an old-fashioned thing. Its pull on our attention is in many respects weak in comparison with the easy entertainments of TV, film, computer games, phones and other teletechnology. More than poems or short stories, the future of the novel seems bound up with that of the book. The book remains an object of affection, but in an increasingly rarefied, circumscribed way. And the book, we tend to think, is a slow thing, even if we also attribute to it (for example on a train journey) the ability to *kill time*.

In truth the novel is a key to the experience and value of speed, and to a critical understanding of those forms of teletechnology in comparison with which it can seem such a tortoise.

Take telephones. Especially in their mobile form, they speed up life and communication, intensify anticipation and knowledge, inject new complexity into postponement and decisions. This presents formidable challenges to 'the novel today'. If you want to write a novel you really have to be engaged (no pun intended). A certain era of literature appears to be over. This was announced, in characteristically playful, downbeat fashion, by the American poet Frank O'Hara when he suggested in a little text called 'Personism', dating from August 1959, that there was no need for him to write a poem; instead he could simply telephone the person he wanted to address. It is not that telephone calls (or, more recently, emails or text messages) replace poems. Telephones don't deplete pleasure, they complicate and can also of course enrich it. More subtly, they interrupt and interfere with the way we desire and think about poetry. And what goes for poetry here also goes for the novel, for any novel worthy of the name is poetic.

Writers have long had a thing about telephones. Mark Twain, Marcel Proust, Franz Kafka and James Joyce, for example, were all fascinated by the strange voice-at-a-distance that a 'telephone' literally is. But O'Hara's Personism represents something new, going to the heart of what we suppose a poem might be or do. His discovery is that the telephone has been installed, there is a poetry of telephony, and no one can really write poems any more without finding themselves – and the value or purpose of their writing – on the line. O'Hara's telephone is an updated version of E. M. Forster's suggestive idea, in *Aspects of the Novel*, that writing a novel is like writing a letter.

How should a novel deal with the reality of telephones and of other, newer modes of telecommunication? To ignore or avoid reference to this reality is obviously one option; but this can inevitably come to look like disavowal or dishonesty. The future of literature is inextricably linked up with these forms of teletechnology, in the most 'wireless' ways conceivable. The novel has to work at new velocities, with new rhythms. It has to break up, interrupt, slow down and reroute unexpectedly. There is little point in supposing that new forms of telecommunication are going to be novel-friendly, or vice versa. The novel has to resist and twist, accommodate and diverge. After all, nothing in a work of fiction dates more quickly than the latest gizmo. A novel wants to be a joy forever, or, let's say, a joy-fever, a fever that resists treatment, that stays with you awhile and can come back, at once chronic and fitful.

You recall the beginning: 'In the middle of the night the phone rings, over and over, but I don't hear it.' The reader hears about what the narrator doesn't hear. It is the novel calling. The novel is a kind of weird telephone exchange. Reality literature would be writing that acknowledges this weirdness and goes somewhere that was not foreseeable, either for the author or for the reader. And at the same time it makes the word 'weird' vibrate with all the resonances of prophecy, fate and clairvoyance we meet with in *Macbeth*'s witches, the never-faraway weird sisters.

Telephones exist in novels long before Alexander Graham Bell and others came along. Wherever you have a narrative or narrator telling you what a character is thinking or feeling, wherever you have someone reportedly thinking to themselves (like Alice in Lewis Carroll), wherever you have a narrator who is not the same as the author, wherever you have a story in which you hear about things which haven't happened yet or which are happening to someone else without their knowledge, you can pick up a sense of the strange telephone network.

When do you get the call?

These things happen from time to time.

You might suppose that reality literature is the first literary genre to be explicitly derived from TV. The phrase 'reality TV' dates back, according to the *Oxford English Dictionary*, to an article published in *Newsweek* in March 1978. Reality TV is of course a fiction. Like everything else on TV that appears to reach us in a natural or unmediated form, whether it is a 'wildlife documentary' or the 'world news', it is constructed, programmed and ethnocentric. *Reality literature* invites us, on the contrary, to be wary of such constructions and narrow-mindedness. It seeks to question and complicate, to dislocate and interfere. Is it a literary reality or a literature *of* reality? 'Reality literature' lives on this duplicity. It is not a genre but something more ghostly and fleeting. Its vivacity is spectral: it knows that the dead speak and that without the completely unexpected openings generated out of mourning there would be no future. It is something that happens, perhaps, when the novel is operating at top speed, gone before you can say.

You might suppose that reality literature entails a new attention to realism, even a new kind of realism. Again, you would be right. Yet the force and focus here is not only realism, but what makes it possible. It is the wayward telephone network. There is a literary telephony or, better perhaps, a literary telepathy, that has to do with the singular nature of magical thinking in literature. To read a novel is to enter a world of magical thinking. (This doesn't mean you're mad or 'believe in superstition' or have to surrender your reason at the door: like love itself, the doorway is magical.) Realism, in this respect, is not so much about credible characters, places, experiences and events, about furniture and food, sadness and street-corners, and so many other narrative details, all or some of which are taken to be suggestive of what is called 'the real world' or 'real life'. Rather, realism is, first of all, what is secured through telepathy and clairvoyance. Reading the thoughts of others, receiving fateful intimations or weird knowledge of the future, hearing what others are feeling: that is what you find yourself doing when you read a novel.

(In a final parenthetical pouch, let me just add: what is at issue here is something ultimately foreign to religion, animism or superstition. The novel would be a space of quilted thinking. *Quilt*'s a queer word, to be sure. It is perhaps the true afterword here, the title-term that came some time after the writing was done, seeming to raise itself up out of the text. It is a matter of reckoning with all its meanings, associations and sounds (*quilt, quill, will, kill, ill, kilt, wilt, quit, it*), with all it covers and uncovers, as well as its distance from a world of simple surfaces and depths, concealment or revelation. What may seem so ordinary quickly becomes odd. You might think of something that you get under, something soft and comfortable, but dictionaries start off curiously abstract. Thus the primary definition in *Chambers*, for example, proceeds: 'quilt *[kwilt] noun*: a bedcover consisting of padding between two outer layers of cloth stitched through all three layers into compartments or channels; any material or piece of material so treated...' Another way of talking about novels is perhaps evoked: instead of 'narrative perspective', 'first person narration', 'indirect discourse', 'point of view', 'focalisation' and so on, there would be layers and pockets of voices, feelings, thoughts. 'Quilt' is also a verb, of course, meaning: to swallow. The principal sense here, however, is as another name – apparently dating from the eighteenth century – for a manta ray.)

Let us turn and begin again, this time without stopping:

In the middle of the night the phone rings, over and over...

'Vivid and visceral, *London Triptych* cuts deep
to reveal the hidden layers of a secret history.'
Jake Arnott

'Charting three very different affairs taking place against
the backdrop of three very different Londons, Jonathan
Kemp's first novel is a thought-provoking enquiry
into what changes in gay men's lives as the decades pass –
and what doesn't. As the connections and reflections
across the years reveal themselves, this is a book that
will make you think – and make you feel.'
Neil Bartlett

Three men, three lives and three eras sinuously entwine
in a dark, startling and unsettling narrative of sex,
exploitation and dependence set against London's
strangely constant gay underworld.

Rent boys and models, aristocrats, artists and gangsters
populate this bold début as the lives and loves of three men
interweave in three distinct and pertinent historical periods.

ISBN: 978-0-9562515-3-4

MORE FROM MYRIAD EDITIONS

'Lyrical, warm and moving, this impressive début
is reminiscent of Laurie Lee.'
Meera Syal

'A funny, moving and quirky coming-of-age story.
Hugely enjoyable.'
Deborah Moggach

Ellis is obsessed by the spiders that inhabit the family's
crumbling house – and also by a need to find out more
about his mother, whose death overshadows the family's
otherwise happy existence.

Against the vividly described background of 1980s rural
Kent, this moving portrait of a father-son relationship
shifts effortlessly between evoking utterly convincingly
the terrors and joys of adolescence and the pleasure
and pain of being an adult.

ISBN: 978-0-9562515-2-7

MORE FROM MYRIAD EDITIONS

**Selected for
Waterstone's New Voices 2010**

Set during the first Australian cricket tour of England
in 1868, this magnificent novel explores an extraordinary
friendship between one of the Aboriginal players and
a young woman whose quiet routine takes on
a new aspect when the cricketer arrives on her doorstep.

From Lord's cricket ground to the banks of the Thames
at Shadwell, they follow the trail of Joseph Druce,
a convicted felon transported to New South Wales
eighty years earlier.

Taking its lead from true historical events, Ed Hillyer has
created an epic brimming with memorable characters,
historical intrigue and documentary detail.

ISBN: 978-0-9562515-0-3

MORE FROM MYRIAD EDITIONS

An Orwellian dystopia in the guise of a fast-paced
thriller, this is a coolly satirical novel laced with
humour, suspense and intrigue.

After years of civil conflict, gated communities
separate government workers from the Scoomers
cruising the streets in their battered Fiats. But when
Jack and Denise witness a fatal car crash one night,
this precarious security is ruptured.

Through conversations between characters, leaked
tapes of official meetings, transcribed phone calls,
fly posters for prayer meetings, and provocative articles
in an illegal newspaper, this haunting vision of corruption
and surveillance is at once deeply unsettling and
frighteningly familiar.

ISBN: 978-0-9562515-1-0

MORE FROM MYRIAD EDITIONS

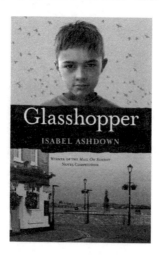

'Tender and subtle, it explores difficult issues in deceptively easy prose... Across the decades, Ashdown tiptoes carefully through explosive family secrets. This is a wonderful début – intelligent, understated and sensitive.'
Observer

'An intelligent, beautifully observed coming-of-age story, packed with vivid characters and inch-perfect dialogue. Isabel Ashdown's storytelling skills are formidable; her human insights highly perceptive.'
Mail on Sunday

'Isabel Ashdown's first novel is a disturbing, thought-provoking tale of family dysfunction, spanning the second half of the 20th century, that guarantees laughter at the uncomfortable familiarity of it all.'
'Best Books of the Year', *London Evening Standard*

'An immaculately written novel with plenty of dark family secrets and gentle wit within. Recommended for book groups.'
Waterstone's Books Quarterly

ISBN: 978-0-9549309-7-4

'One of those brilliant books that offers an easy, entertaining
read in the first instance, only to worm its way deeper into your
mind. A modern Graham Greene – fabulous... fictional gold.'
Argus

'Graham Greene-ish with a bit of Alexander McCall Smith
thrown in. Very readable, very humorous – a charming
first novel.'
Radio 5 Live Up All Night

'This fascinating novel is clearly the work of a very professional
author, who brings to it a knowing, beady eye and an acute
understanding of the use of irony. Entertaining and rewarding,
it is rich in dialogue and her characters are finely and sensitively
drawn. Sue Eckstein is to be congratulated on an excellent
début. If you like Armistead Maupin, Graham Greene or
Barbara Trapido, you will love this.'
bookgroup.info

'Populated by a cast of miscreants and misfits
this is a darkly comic delight.'
Choice

ISBN: 978-0-9549309-8-1

MORE FROM MYRIAD EDITIONS

'Thomson skilfully evokes the era and the slow-moving
quality of childhood summers, suggesting the menace
lurking just beyond the vision of her young protagonists.
A study of memory and guilt with several twists.'
Guardian

'This emotionally charged thriller grips from the first
paragraph, and a nail-biting level of suspense is maintained
throughout. A great second novel.'
She

'Such is the vividness of the descriptions of the location
in this well structured and well written novel that I want
to get the next train down. On the edge of my seat?
No way – I was cowering under it.'
shotsmag.co.uk

ISBN: 978-0-9549309-4-3

MORE FROM MYRIAD EDITIONS

'Martine McDonagh writes with a cool, clear confidence about a world brought to its knees. Her protagonist, a woman living alone but battling on into the future, is utterly believable, as are her observations of the sodden landscape she finds herself inhabiting. This book certainly got under my skin – if you like your books dark and more than a little disturbing, this is one for you.'
Mick Jackson

'An exquisitely crafted début novel set in a post-apocalyptic landscape. I'm rationing myself to five pages per day in order to make it last.'
Guardian Unlimited

'An all-too-convincing picture of life…in the middle of this century – cold and stormy, with most modern conveniences long-since gone, and with small, mainly self-sufficient communities struggling to maintain a degree of social order. It is very atmospheric…leaves an indelible imprint on the psyche.'
BBC Radio 4 Open Book

ISBN: 978-0-9549309-2-9

MORE FROM MYRIAD EDITIONS

This celebration of Brighton and Brightonians – resident, itinerant and visiting – is a feast of words and pictures specially commissioned from established artists and emerging talents.

'*The Brighton Book* is a fantastic idea and I loved writing a piece with crazy wonderful Brighton as the theme. Everybody should buy the book because it's such a great mix of energy and ideas.'
Jeanette Winterson

'Packed with unique perspectives on the city... *The Brighton Book* has hedonism at its heart. Give a man a fish and you'll feed him for a day. Give him *The Brighton Book* and you will feed him for a lifetime.'
Argus

Contributors: Melissa Benn, Louis de Bernières, Piers Gough, Roy Greenslade, Bonnie Greer, Lee Harwood, Mick Jackson, Lenny Kaye, Nigella Lawson, Martine McDonagh, Boris Mikhailov, Woodrow Phoenix, John Riddy, Meg Rosoff, Miranda Sawyer, Posy Simmonds, Ali Smith, Catherine Smith, Diana Souhami, Lesley Thomson, Jeanette Winterson.

ISBN: 978-0-9549309-0-5